CHARMED,
I'M SURE

ALADDIN

An imprint of Simon & Schuster Children's Publishing Division

1230 Avenue of the Americas, New York, New York 10020

First Aladdin hardcover edition September 2016

Text copyright © 2016 by Sarah Darer Littman

Cover illustration copyright © 2016 by Angela Navarra

All rights reserved, including the right of reproduction in whole or in part in any form.

ALADDIN is a trademark of Simon & Schuster, Inc., and related logo is a registered trademark of Simon & Schuster, Inc.

For information about special discounts for bulk purchases, please contact Simon & Schuster Special Sales at 1-866-506-1949 or business@simonandschuster.com.

The Simon & Schuster Speakers Bureau can bring authors to your live event. For more information or to book an event contact the Simon & Schuster Speakers Bureau at 1-866-248-3049 or visit our website at www.simonspeakers.com.

Book designed by Laura Lyn DiSiena

The text of this book was set in Bembo Infant.

Manufactured in the United States of America 0816 FFG

10 9 8 7 6 5 4 3 2 1

Library of Congress Control Number 2015956906

ISBN 978-1-4814-5127-7 (hc)

ISBN 978-1-4814-5128-4 (eBook)

CHARMED, I'M SURE

◈ SARAH DARER LITTMAN ◈

ALADDIN
New York London Toronto Sydney New Delhi

To Cindy Beth Minnich—teacher, Nerdy Book Club goddess, and friend—for helping me to find the key to this story . . . finally!

Meanwhile Snow White held court,
rolling her china-blue doll eyes open and shut
and sometimes referring to her mirror
as women do.

—"SNOW WHITE AND THE SEVEN DWARFS"
BY ANNE SEXTON (1928–1974)

Chapter One

I AM NOW OFFICIALLY A LOSER.

Thirty seconds ago, my best friend Katie announced that Quinn Fairchild asked her to the Fall Festive. Last week Dave Theis asked my other best friend, Nicole. Which leaves me as the only one of my friends without a date.

What makes it worse is that I'm the sole heir of two of the most famous people in fairy tale history. You may have heard of them: Snow White and Prince Charming.

The Charming name comes with some serious baggage. Especially when you're an eighth grader at the Manhattan World Themes Middle School, there's a dance in two weeks' time, and you don't have a date.

You, the one whose mom was so beautiful that her step-mother went on a killing spree just so she could reclaim the title of Fairest in the Land as judged by some crazy talking mirror. You, the one whose prince of a father literally rode in on a white horse to start their happily ever after.

Yep, that's me. Rosamunde White Charming. My friends call me Rosie.

But now isn't the time to indulge in self-pity. Now is the time to be happy for Katie, because she *does* have a date, namely Quinn Fairchild, whom she has been crushing on forever.

"That's the best news!" I tell Katie. Which it is, for her. Personally, I'm not a big fan of Quinn Fairchild. He's a little (okay, a lot) too full of himself. But if going to the Fall Festive with him makes Katie happy, what kind of friend would I be if I weren't happy for her?

"I know!" Katie sighs. Her face takes on the same dreamy glow Mom's does when she tells The Tale of how she and Dad met. "I've been waiting for this day since I saw him the first day of sixth grade. And now it's finally happened."

"I just hope he's worth the wait," I say.

Katie's dreamy glow disappears.

"Sheesh, Rosie. Just because you were born without the romance gene, it doesn't mean you have to rain on Katie's parade," Nicole says.

"I didn't mean to," I protest.

"Well, you did," Katie snaps. "A big, gray, damp cloud of precipitation, right in the middle of my happy marching band."

"Sorry," I mumble.

"It's okay," Katie says. She gives me a concerned, pitying look. "Are you stressed out about finding a date?"

She's half-right, so I might as well take the lifeline she's thrown me.

"Yeah. I guess."

"I know! You should go with Quinn's friend Hunter," Katie exclaims. "It would be fun to double date. Plus, he's cute and you'd look great in pictures together."

Hunter Farthington is the star striker on the soccer team. The problem is that I sit behind him in social studies, and let's just say that while I can't argue with the cute part, he's not the sharpest tool in the Manhattan World Themes Middle School shed. He thinks people from Denmark are called "Great Danes."

"Who cares?" Katie says when I tell her this and explain that, no, he was serious, not joking, and actually argued with the teacher about it because he was so convinced he was right. "It's a dance, not a debate, Rosie."

"But we won't be dancing all the time. I've got nothing to say to him. All he ever talks about is soccer and what famous people he's seen on the street and harassed till they took a selfie with him."

"Just pretend," Katie says. "Ask him what he thinks about last night's game. That way, it doesn't matter whether it's football or basketball, hockey or baseball season. There's always some kind of game going on somewhere."

"Why do I have to pretend to be interested in something he likes just to get a date?" I ask. "Shouldn't he pretend to be interested in me, too? Is being fake the way to get a guy to like me?"

"You're totally overthinking this, Rosie," Katie says. "It's a problem you have. Think of it this way: He's a boy, he's cute, and he can dance. Make it happen."

Like that's so easy.

"I think you might be better off with Damien Wolfe," Nicole argues. "He's more your type. You'd make such a cute couple."

Damien's in my math class. He always sits in the back

row, his dark hair brushing over the collar of his leather jacket as he bends forward over his notebook, scribbling intently with black pen. He draws. Really well, in fact. Damien definitely seems interesting. There's just one slight problem. I've barely spoken three words to him in my life. He's super quiet and I've never been assigned to work with him on a project. So . . . yeah. About three words. Maybe five. Plus a few passing head nods in the hall. His hair moves nicely when he nods his head—I'll give him that.

Still . . .

"How do you *know* he's my type?" I ask Nicole.

"He . . . just is," she says. That's a big help.

"Ask him to the dance. You won't regret it," Nicole declares.

Considering I've never been on an actual date, or even had a real crush, I don't get how she can know "my type." *I* haven't even figured it out yet.

"Now that we've solved Rosie's date problem, can we get back to the matter at hand?" Katie says.

"Which is . . . ?" I inquire.

"Dress shopping," she announces. "On Saturday. I need your expert opinions."

Fashion isn't my area of expertise, but hanging out with my friends is.

"Works for me," I say.

"Sounds like a plan," Nicole agrees.

"I'll make a list of stores," Katie says.

Knowing Katie, this shopping trip is going to be planned with the detail and precision of a major military campaign. *Note to self: Wear comfortable shoes and bring snacks.*

While I listen to my friends discussing dresses and dates, I'm conscious that time is ticking by, and I have neither.

That's when I decide I'm desperate enough to do something that I promised myself I would never do, because all previous attempts have ended so badly:

I'm going to ask my mother for advice.

Chapter Two

WHEN I GET HOME FROM SCHOOL, MOM IS in her home office, working on a new piece for her website, CharmingLifestyles.com.

Here's one of the typical posts on the site: *You too can meet your Prince Charming: 12 Easy Steps to Make It Happen!* I didn't read it, but I could write that article in my sleep:

1) Charming men love charming ladies. Mind your manners!

2) Get your beauty rest! The sleepy dwarf look won't cut it.

3) Moisturize, moisturize, moisturize, and minimize!

The secret to dewy, flawless "skin like snow" is a night cream that won't quit.

4) Don't be bashful! Men like confident women.

5) Smile and radiate positivity! Princes don't go for grumpy gals.

6) Take CynCorp brand vitamins—available right here on CharmingLifestyles.com—to keep your body healthy. Sneezing is *not* sexy!

7) Read the Charming Lifestyles News section to stay *au courant*. The last thing you want is to sound dopey on a date!

8) An apple a day keeps the doc away and helps with maintaining a figure to die for!

9) Keep your hair shiny, lustrous, and tangle free with The Magic Comb™—buy one today and get a free StaySvelte™ bodyshaper with purchase!

10) Be happy—laughter is contagious!

11) Pucker up for True Love's Kiss with our special Lips as Red as Blood™ moisturizing lip stain. Your prince will be smitten for life!

12) Live happily ever after—and *CharmingLifestyles.com will help you find out how*!

Of course, Mom would *never* post the *real* way she and Dad hooked up:

1) Make your stepmother mad. Like, *seriously angry*.
2) Convince the guy who is supposed to kill you and bring her your heart to let you go and to kill a deer instead. (*"What? You made him kill Bambi?"* I asked when I was younger, before launching into a tantrum about my mother's cruelty to animals.)
3) Run away.
4) Break into somebody's house.
5) Get your OCD on and clean the filthy place. Even though it's *not your house and you don't even know who lives there.*
6) Agree to be unpaid domestic help for a bunch of "height disadvantaged" men in return for food and lodging.
7) Despite the obvious Stranger Danger, buy a hair comb from a rando because you are obsessed with how you look, even though the only people who see you are the aforementioned bunch of short dudes.
8) Almost die. Saved by clumsy, height disadvantaged man knocking comb out of your hair.
9) Refuse to learn from your mistakes. Buy apple from another stranger.
10) Choke on poisoned apple and die. Get buried in a glass coffin because all the height disadvantaged

men will, quote, "miss seeing your beautiful face." Which is beyond weird, if you ask me, because we learned in science that your body is going to start decomposing. So . . . gross!

11) Wait until some random dude rides or drives by (white horse or sports car preferred), becomes entranced by your beauty, opens the coffin, and kisses you (so wrong, *amirite?*), thereby dislodging the piece of poison apple and magically waking you, because you're not actually dead, you're merely in an extremely deep sleep that makes it look that way. That's the excuse and you're both sticking to it.

12) Live happily ever after—and CharmingLifestyles .com WILL HELP YOU FIND OUT HOW! (Not to mention selling you a whole bunch of *stuff* that you'll need to do it. . . .)

Thanks to an investment from the international manufacturing conglomerate CynCorp, Mom and Dad have built up a lucrative business empire around the Charming brand and CharmingLifestyles.com. Mom's got her own range of beauty and antiaging products (*Guaranteed to make sure you stay the Fairest in the Land, no matter what the mirror says!* according to the infomercial). Dad has a range of sporting goods and luxury accessories. (*Steal her heart with The Huntsman bow and arrow!* and *It'll be love at first sight when you wear Prince Charming leather boots.*) Dad's in charge of sales and marketing. He doesn't trust Mom out on the road, because she's too trusting of strangers.

They argue about that. Constantly.

"That was once, once upon a time!" Mom protests.

"Actually, it was twice," Dad always reminds her. "And you'd still be lying in that glass sarcophagus surrounded by a bunch of morose dwarves if I hadn't come along."

"How do you know?" Mom argues. "I'm sure some *other* handsome prince would have come along eventually. . . ."

And then Dad gets jealous and it goes on from there, getting more and more heated till eventually they kiss and make up. *Barf.*

Anyway, after getting a snack, I go into Mom's office and slump into one of the armchairs opposite her desk.

She looks up briefly.

"Hi, honey. How was school?"

"Educational," I say. Mom's used to me giving her noncommittal answers about school, and because she's involved in her work, she doesn't press me further.

I almost decide not to ask her. *She's busy. . . . I don't want to interrupt her.*

Besides, Mom's solutions to my everyday teenage problems can lead to mega-embarrassment. Like when I told her I had cramps, she couldn't just say, *Here's a hot water bottle and some ibuprofen*, like a *normal* mom. Instead, she dragged me to the New York Botanical Garden in the Bronx, where she not very surreptitiously stole red raspberry leaves, horsetail, and yarrow to make me a *decoction*. A security guard yelled at her for picking the plants, but Mom smiled at him, gave him the full force of her Fairest in the Land face, pointed to me, and said that it was a matter of urgent necessity because of my *cramps*. She whispered the word "cramps," but it didn't matter, I still wanted to die from embarrassment on the spot.

Still, the dance is getting closer and I'm a dateless Charming. Desperate times call for desperate measures.

"Mom, the Fall Festive dance is in two weeks, and I don't have a date. Do you have any suggestions?"

I've uttered two magic words to get her complete attention: "dance" and "date." Oh, make that three: "*suggestions*." Her whole website is built around suggesting to people how to better live their life the Charming way.

Mom gives me her assessing look. Right this minute if you gave me the choice between taking my chance on my stepgrandma's talking mirror and my mother's *let's take a look at Rosie and see what we can do with her* stare, I'd take the whacked-out mirror in a heartbeat. And that's knowing how the story ended.

"Oh, Rosamunde, I've been waiting for this day for such a long time," Mom says, getting all dewy-eyed.

"What day?" I ask warily.

"The day you finally ask me for advice," she says. "Of course I'm here for you, my dearest daughter. I always am and always will be. And there's *so much* we can do!"

Why am I suddenly getting the sneaking suspicion that asking the doyenne of Being the Best You Gets the Best Out of Him might not have been the wisest decision I've ever made?

But then Mom gets up from behind her desk and hugs me.

"Come with me, sweetheart. There's something special I want to give you."

I follow her down the hallway from her office to the dressing room off my parents' bedroom. Mom's dressing room is bigger than a lot of people's studio apartments in Manhattan. Seriously, she could probably rent it out for over $1,500 a month.

Mom doesn't do well in small spaces—I think it's something to do with the whole glass coffin thing. Apparently, it took years of therapy and some of Herb the Dwarf's special antianxiety tonic before she could get into the elevator at our apartment building without having a major anxiety attack. Once, when she was pregnant with me, Dad had to carry her up the stairs. He was saying some less than Charming things by the time he got to our front door, or so I'm told.

Besides Mom's extensive collection of dresses, shoes, and accessories, the dressing room features a gilt-framed full-length mirror (it doesn't talk, as far as I know, which is a relief, because that didn't do Stepgrandma a whole lot of good) and, behind that, a safe.

You'd think coming from our fairy tale background it would open with some magic spell, but instead of "Abracadabra" or "Open sesame," it requires a boring old combination.

Mom spins the dial and opens it, then rummages around amid all the important papers, passports, family jewels (for reals, we're talking actual *crowns* and *tiaras* and stuff) until she finds a small black velvet pouch.

She closes the safe, returns the mirror to position, and then turns to me, her eyes glistening.

"Rosamunde, I've been waiting for the right time to

give this to you. And now is that time," she says, holding out the velvet pouch.

I can't help noticing that even when she gets all teared up, Mom looks beautiful. Her tears are like Swarovski crystals, setting off the sapphire blue of her eyes. I wonder if she ever does the red-eyed, *snot pouring out of the nose* thing like Katie, Nicole, and I do when we watch sad movies.

The velvet bag slides into my hand, heavy and warm. I open it and out slides a gold compact, embossed with my mother's family coat of arms and inlaid with precious stones—diamonds, rubies, emeralds, and sapphires.

"Wow!" I exclaim. "It's . . . beautiful!"

I touch a ruby with my fingertip. It seems to glow with an internal fire, but the stone is cool.

"Don't you think it's a little . . . you know . . . *fancy* for me?" I ask Mom. "It must be worth lots of money. What happens if I lose it?"

My mother takes my face in her cool, white as snow fingers, nails painted Red as Blood (of course).

"You are a princess of the royal blood, Rosamunde," she says. Her gaze drops to my less than princessy outfit of jeans, T-shirt, and Converse. "You may try to hide behind your grungy T-shirts and those laceless sneakers, but your lineage will not be forsworn. Blood will out, as they say."

I have no idea what she means by that, but I'm too distracted by the bling to ask any more questions, so I open the compact, which seems to grow heavier the longer I hold it in my hand.

Everyday Rosie Charming stares back at me. I've got my dad's brown hair and my mom's blue eyes. The big chin zit, alas, is all mine.

What will it take to make you understand that you could be the Fairest in the Land?

The words are so quiet I'm not sure I actually heard them. I can't believe Mom would use that line on me, of all people.

"Wait, what?" I ask.

"I didn't say anything," Mom tells me. "But I think if you take a good look at yourself, you'll agree that maybe a little"—she hesitates, trying to find the Charming way to put it—"*styling* might be in order."

Fairest in the Land . . . Rosamunde . . . Fairest in the Land . . .

There it is again. I look around Mom's dressing room but there's no one here but us.

It's official. Finding a date for the Fall Festive is making me crazy.

"So, what do you think, Rosie?" Mom asks.

"Think about what?"

"My suggestion. Let's get you a little help with styling so you can put your best dating self forward," Mom says. She's already got her cell phone in hand, ready to start making calls to set the beautifying process in motion.

"Can you define 'styling'?"

"Nothing much," she says. "Just the teensiest makeover. I'll see if Phillipe can fit you in tomorrow afternoon. I'll tell him it's an emergency."

"Wait," I say as she's about to press speed dial. "Why is it always about how I look?"

Her finger pauses over the button on the phone, and she looks at me as if I'm simple.

"Because the fairest one of all gets the prince, Rosie," Mom explains as if I'm a three-year-old who has forgotten her ABCs. "Remember how Dad and I met."

She's got that misty look in her eyes, the one she always gets when she tells The Tale.

Like I could ever forget it.

"I opened my eyes and saw your father's face and knew, right away, that we would be together forever."

Everyone knows my parents' story, and no one else seems to be freaked out by it the way I am. Every time I imagine being totally passed out and waking up to find some strange guy kissing me, all I think is "EWW, NOPE! NOPE! NOPE!" So what if he's really good-looking? I can't see how Romance could outweigh the Creeper Factor.

I wonder, not for the first time, if there's something wrong with me. Maybe I'm some kind of mutant who's missing the romantic gene.

"But . . . how did you know he was your true love from one kiss?" I persist. "I mean, you got lucky . . . we got lucky . . . because Dad's awesome, but what if he'd turned out to be a complete jerk?"

Mom throws her head back and laughs. Her laugh is musical, like the tinkling of water as it pours over cut crystal.

"That wouldn't happen. . . . Your father is a *prince*."

Mom says it like my father's royal blood automatically means that he is incapable of doing anything wrong, ever. But I read history books as well as fairy tales. And let me tell you, there are princes who weren't nearly as charming as Dad. Not by a long shot. Take Richard, who murdered his two nephews in the tower, so he could become King Richard III of England. Or the other English prince who became King Henry VIII. He decided he didn't like two of his wives, so he chopped off their heads. Now *there's* a keeper. . . .

But Mom's got that gooey-eyed look again, which means there's no point using logic with her.

"I'll take care of this," she says, pressing Phillipe's speed dial number. "Don't worry, Rosie. We'll get you a date for the dance." She smiles at me, the lovey-dovey look still intact. "And you'll find your own Prince Charming someday too."

"That's what I'm afraid of," I mutter as I escape to my bedroom to research solutions of my own.

Back in my room I decide that since my friends haven't been that much help with finding a date, I might as well try technology.

"How do I get a date?" I ask the intelligent personal assistant in my phone.

"Hold on a minute, I'm just checking that for you," she says in her weird, computer-generated voice.

She comes up with three dating services for grown-ups. One is for rich, Ivy League educated grown-ups. Not exactly what I'm looking for as a date to Fall Festive.

I think my "intelligent" personal assistant isn't that

bright or she needs a hearing aid. Whenever I ask her to call Nicole, she replies: "Paul a hole?"

Sighing, I open my laptop and google *How to get a date in middle school.*

There's actually a step-by-step guide. *Yes!* Who needs a fairy godmother when you've got the Internet?

Or at least that's what I think until I read step one.

Be charming and funny—but not too flirtatious or you might get a reputation you don't want. Be confident. But don't come across as loud and strident. Otherwise, guys might think you're a thing that rhymes with witch.

What does that even *mean?* I think there's some evil crone in a room somewhere making this stuff up so that dateless girls get confused and crazy. I can't bring myself to read any more. It's enough to make me wish I had a real fairy godmother.

Being the first dateless Charming is looking better all the time. But now that I've told Mom, I doubt I'll be allowed that option.

Chapter Three

MOM MANAGES TO SWING AN EMERGENCY appointment for me after school the next day with Phillipe, the personal stylist at Très Cher department store, to whom she refers all her top tier Charming Lifestyles subscribers. So I don't bother going home; I head to Starcups for a skinny mocha instead. I nab one of the armchairs near the window and pull out *Romeo and Juliet*, a notebook, and a pen. It figures we're doing some *love at first sight* Shakespeare play in Language Arts when I'm dateless, doesn't it?

Still, look how well the whole *true love* thing worked out for those two lovebirds. They ended up dead and deader.

I'd be happy to swear off romance forever, if I weren't Rosie Charming with a family legacy to uphold. Besides, I've got to write a three page response about Romeo and Juliet's crazy doomed love by Thursday.

Romeo and Juliet are referred to as "star-cross'd lovers." I don't understand why this play is considered so romantic. Romeo is an inconsistent, egotistical flake, and Juliet only falls for him because he's good-looking and she's too sheltered to know any better. One minute Romeo is head over heels in love with Rosaline and moping around with his Montague buddies because she doesn't love him back, and then boom! He sees Juliet once and suddenly he's forgotten that Rosaline ever existed, and he's literally climbing the walls to talk to Juliet on her balcony.

It makes you wonder if Romeo even knows what real love is, or if he's just in love with the idea of it. All it takes is for the next beautiful girl to come along and he's ready to transfer his affections.

"See, how she leans her cheek upon her hand! O, that I were a glove upon that hand, That I might touch that cheek!"

I look up, startled. Is Romeo actually here somewhere?

There's a guy who looks to be about my age standing next to the chair opposite me. He's tall and lanky with dark hair that hangs over his eyes. He's wearing black straight-leg jeans and a T-shirt with a grumpy-looking cartoon skunk who's saying *Love Stinks*. He's also smiling at me. The guy, not the skunk, that is.

He points to my copy of *Romeo and Juliet*.

"What do you think of the Bard?" he asks.

I shrug.

"He's okay. I liked *A Midsummer Night's Dream* better. I'm not a big Romeo fan."

"Okay if I sit here?" he says.

I shrug. "Suit yourself."

"So, what have you got against my man R. Montague?" he asks, leaning forward. I notice that he's doodled some cool geometric designs on the sides of his Converse in black Sharpie.

"The guy says he's in love, but how do you go from being lovesick over Rosaline to head over heels in love with Juliet in one night?" I ask. "It's ridiculous. I mean, seriously, if I were Juliet, I wouldn't trust the guy, much less *kill myself* over him."

"Maybe he just *thought* he was in love with Rosaline," Mystery Shakespeare Boy says.

"So, what if he just *thought* he was in love with Juliet and drank the poison because he's an emo drama queen."

Mystery Shakespeare Boy laughs, revealing that he

(a) has already had his braces off and (b) has nice teeth.

"Wow, you're a tough customer, Miss *I Don't Believe in Romance*."

I glance pointedly at his T-shirt.

"*I'm* not the one wearing a *Love Stinks* T-shirt."

"You got me there," he admits with a grin. "So . . . what's your opinion on Miz Juliet Capulet?"

"She's never had a chance to live. She's so sheltered. I mean, the girl still has a nurse," I explain. "And then this smooth-talking hottie puts the moves on her. . . . Well, even though I think she's crazy, I don't blame her as much as Romeo."

"So you're a guy hater, huh?"

"I am not!" I protest. "Romeo's just . . . shallow and immature."

"Not that you're judgmental or anything."

He's starting to annoy me. I am so *not* judgmental. . . . Am I?

I make a point of looking at the time on my cell.

"I've got to go," I say, gathering up my books and stuffing them in my bag without looking at him. "I've got a—"

No way am I going to tell Mystery Shakespeare Boy

that my mother has prescribed me what basically boils down to a top-to-toe makeover so I can get a date to the school dance.

"Um . . . a hair . . . appointment."

"Hey, I know it's none of my business," he says, "but I . . . think your hair looks really pretty the way it is."

I'd been swinging my backpack onto my shoulder, and it slams against my side with a heavy thump as I turn to face him, stunned. Boys don't come out and *say* stuff like that. Not in real life. Not to me.

I have no idea what to say back to him. So I stand there like a complete idiot, staring at his face, which I notice is starting to flush. Mumbling, "Gotta go," I bolt for the door.

I hear him call, "Wait—what's your . . ." as the door closes and I exit onto the street. As much as I want to, I don't look back.

Phillipe, my mother's makeover guru, doesn't share Mystery Shakespeare Boy's opinion of my hair. Or my clothes. Or my skin. Or my nails. There doesn't seem to be much about me that Phillipe thinks is pretty.

"*Quelle horreur!*" he says. "But *ne t'inquiètes pas,*

Mademoiselle Rosamunde. By the time Phillipe is finished with you, the young men, they will be lining up
to ask you to the dance!"

Great. My reputation has preceded me. Apparently,
every member of Phillipe's staff knows about my lack of
date prospects for this dance.

Not only that, they've already discussed my hair
beautification plan too. Apparently, I don't get a say,
even though it's my head. I just get to enjoy the smell of
chemicals and the sight of myself looking like a Martian
with twists of aluminum foil all over my skull.

I take a selfie and send it to Nicole and Katie.

Date Material yet?

LOL! Katie texts back.

HAWT! Nicole writes.

Met a cute but annoying guy in Starcups, I text them.

OMG! You cannot date a rando from Starcups! Katie texts
back right away.

Stranger Danger!! Stranger Danger!!!!!! Nicole warns.

Don't worry. I'm not my mom, I text back to them. *I
didn't even tell him my name.*

Good Girl! Katie texts. *Stay safe! And make sure to send
us the After shots.*

I've got Romeo and Juliet and my notebook on my

lap, because thanks to the Starcups guy, I didn't finish my essay. But Phillipe dumps a bunch of glossy hairstyle magazines on top of them and tells me to browse for ideas.

"I just want a trim," I tell him. "I don't want anything too out there."

Phillipe gives a shrug and mutters something under his breath. He says it in French, and I take Spanish, but the tone sounds like my mom when I've disappointed her with my fashion choices again.

Then he gives a stream of instructions in rapid-fire Italian to the hairstylist, Giacomo. When I look in the mirror, they're both nodding in agreement and smiling. I know I'm in danger, because I'm stuck in this chair with tin foil twisties all over my head and Giacomo is the one with the scissors.

I put the magazines aside and open *Romeo and Juliet*, deciding to reread the parts where the two meet and the balcony scene. It's all about love at first sight, just like The Tale of Mom and Dad.

So is this the lesson I'm supposed to be taking away from this: that if you want the kind of love that people read about forever, you have to be passionate but totally clueless?

"*Zis* is why you are such a state, Rosamunde!" Phillipe complains, pulling Shakespeare from my hands. "You spend too much time with your nose in a book and not enough time looking at *ze* pimples on your nose."

What pimples on my nose? I thought I had zits only on my chin!

I look up in the mirror, panicked.

Phillipe lifts my hand and shows it to the manicurist.

"Do *ze* best you can," he says with the kind of tragic import usually reserved for funeral directors.

"After *zis, ze* makeup," he says. "And then, clothes." Phillipe shudders again as he surveys my outfit, the one I'd felt perfectly great in until now. "We *must* do something about your clothes! *Quelle horreur!*"

Deprived of my book, a magazine, or even music, I figure I might as well give in. I close my eyes and let them get on with working their magic.

After the color is rinsed out of my hair and I'm brought back to the Makeover Chair, I hear snipping. Lots of it. Meanwhile, my nails are picked and buffed and my hands drenched in moisturizer and put in heated mitts. Then the pulling, blow-drying, and brushing starts on my head. The mitts are taken off, my hands are wiped down with heated towels, and the manicurist tells me to keep my hands still while she paints my nails.

"What do you think I'm going to do? It's not like I

can do too much with them while you guys are working on me, right?" I say.

"This one needs a personality makeover," Giacomo mutters.

I'm tempted to tell him I heard that, but I don't, because right now I'm feeling more like a widget on a production line than Rosie White Charming. And widgets don't talk.

When my nails are done, the manicurist gives me strict instructions to stay still. Giacomo announces he is finished, and I can open my eyes now to see how much more "*bella*" I look.

"*Non!*" Phillipe says. "Wait till after the makeup for the full effect!"

So I stay still like a good store mannequin, eyes closed, while Kara the makeup artist plucks, paints, brushes, and puffs.

"There," she says after applying lip gloss. "Much better."

"*C'est formidable!*" Phillipe exclaims. "You wouldn't know it was the same *gamine* who walked in here. Open your eyes, Mademoiselle Rose, and see the transformation!"

Afraid to look, I squint at my reflection in the mirror. Or at least what I think is my reflection, because the girl there doesn't look anything like me. Her hair is cut into long layers, and it's glossy with deep golden highlights in the brown locks. Her chin zits have been covered up and her skin evened out to a dewy gold tone, with rosy tinted cheeks framing her glossy pink lips.

To tell you the truth, she freaks me out a little. To tell you the *honest* truth, she freaks me out a lot.

"Wow. I look like I could be on the cover of *Seventeen* or *Teen Vogue* or something." I lean closer to the mirror to check myself out.

"Not in those clothes," Phillipe sniffs. He nods to Giacomo, who whips off the hairdresser smock. "Come. It's time to see to your wardrobe."

Phillipe escorts me to a private dressing room in the teen department, where he's already had his fashion minions pick out an assortment of outfits for me to try on. Outfits that look nothing like what I would normally wear.

"*Seriously?*" I say. "You expect me to wear something like this to *school?*" as Minion One holds up the first outfit, a flowery miniskirt with a flowing pink top. She has ballet flats in my size to match.

Phillipe puts his hands on his hips and looks at me down his nose, over his very chic titanium frame glasses.

"Mademoiselle Rose . . . do you *want* a date for zis dance or *don't you?*"

Minions One and Two are giving me matching disapproving looks.

"Yes, I do," I sigh. I just wish there were an easier way to get one.

I take the outfit and retreat into the dressing room to try it on. Taking off my normal clothes feels like I'm shedding my skin—at least the skin that hasn't already been transformed by makeup.

When I dress, the girl looking back at me is cute and put together. Everything matches. But she's not me. I mean, she is me, obviously, *duh*, but she doesn't *feel* like me. I take out the little compact that Mom gave me so I can look at the back of the outfit.

Things are working according to plan. A little more work and you'll be Fairest in the Land. . . .

Where did that come from? Did the chemicals they use in my hair go to my brain? The voice sounded like it came from the Mirror in the compact. But that can't be it. Maybe I'm going crazy from being subjected to The Tale one too many times?

Anyway, who wants to be the Fairest in the Land? Not me, that's for sure.

Don't say no before you try it. Especially since your mom is buying it!

Okayyy, this is beyond freaky now. Is this some weird reality TV joke my parents are playing on me as a promotion for CharmingLifestyles.com? I wouldn't put it past them. They can get a little out there when it comes to promoting the Charming brand.

I start looking around the dressing room frantically, searching for hidden cameras.

"We have lots more to try on, mademoiselle," Phillipe calls through the door. "How does that fit?"

I shake my head to clear it, close the compact and put it back in my backpack, and open the dressing room door.

For the first time all day, I get a broad smile of approval from Phillipe.

"*Parfait!* Now you are a worthy heir to *Maman*'s legend," he says, clapping his small hands with excitement. He gestures to Minion Two, who hands me another, equally *not me* outfit to try on.

I don't protest this time. I just take it and do as I'm told.

I've always rebelled against The Tale. But being me hasn't scored me a date for the dance. Maybe this crazy inner voice I keep hearing is right, and it's time to embrace the legend instead of fighting it.

Chapter Four

I NEEDED ONLY ONE OR TWO OUTFITS, BUT after seeing me, Phillipe called Mom and persuaded her my dress sense is so appalling that I need a completely new wardrobe with precise instructions on how to wear every item of clothing. Apparently, I am "a danger to (my) fashionable self." The Minions take pictures of me in each outfit and then more pictures of how different outfits can be mixed and matched. Nothing is left to my imagination, "because, *ma petite*, let's face it, when it comes to fashion, your imagination is . . . shall we say . . . lacking?" Phillipe points out.

Since I've decided to give in and embrace the legend, I ignore his insult and bite the side of my cheek to contain the sass. I even manage to pull off the hint of a smile.

"It must be all that time I waste reading books," I say sweetly.

Okay, a little sass leaks out. Nobody's perfect.

Phillipe doesn't even notice.

"*Vraiment!*" he agrees, and the Minions nod like two matching bobbleheads.

They *actually took me seriously* when I said reading books was a waste of time. This day is getting more surreal by the minute.

The Minions pack up a week's worth of outfits for me to carry home, and Phillipe arranges for the rest to be sent to our apartment. He won't let me change back into my jeans and T-shirt.

"If I had my way, I would put these in *ze* garbage"—he pronounces it *gar-bahge*—"but since I don't have my way, I forbid you to wear them except in the privacy of your home. *Nevaire, nevaire*, in public."

He gets so worked up with his "nevers," or "*nevaires*," I worry that if I slip up and wear my jeans—or accidentally wear the top of one outfit with the bottom of another—that the cosmic disturbance to Phillipe's world will be so great he'll implode into a quivering mass of Gallic goop.

The responsibility lies heavy on my shoulders.

"Now go, *ma chérie*," Phillipe says, kissing one hand as Minion Two comes and places the heavy shopping bag in the other. "Make us proud."

I smile, weakly, and promise to do my best. Phillipe reminds me about my posture. "Wings back, chest out!" he commands, and sends me on my way.

As soon as I emerge from the revolving doors of Très Cher, something is different. It takes three blocks for me to figure out what it is. I might be on the honor roll at school, but when it comes to this stuff, I'll be the first to admit I'm clueless.

The first thing I notice is the smiling. As any native New Yorker knows, people never smile during rush hour, especially at a teenager with a backpack and a big shopping bag impeding their progress toward the nearest subway entrance. But people *are* smiling at me. I wonder if there's something funny about the way I look, like maybe I accidentally tucked the skirt in my underwear when I went to the bathroom before I left the store.

I glance at my reflection in a store window and get a shock. Not because my skirt *is* accidentally tucked up in my underwear, but because the girl I'm used to seeing isn't there—and the girl I do see is someone I'd probably check out too. There's something about her that draws the eye.

The Fairest in the Land . . .

I shake my head, turning away from my reflection.

Why do I keep hearing things? Maybe all the chemicals from the highlighting are affecting my brain. Or maybe I'm allergic to all this makeup. Whatever it is, it's freaking me out.

"Hey, what's happening?"

A guy about my age starts walking next to me and chatting as if we know each other, except I've never seen him before in my life.

"Uh . . . nothing much," I say, glancing at him briefly and then looking away.

"How's your day been?" he asks.

Why does he want to know? Why does he care? We just met five seconds ago. And technically we haven't, really.

"Okay," I say. *Well, except that all these people are smiling at me during rush hour, which is weird, and now some random guy on the street is talking to me, which is even weirder.*

I kind of want to ignore him and hope he goes away, but I can hear my mother's voice saying: *Charming men love charming ladies. Mind your manners!* So I ask him how *his* day has been, even though I don't particularly want to know the answer because *I don't even know you, random dude walking next to me.*

"It's awesome, now that I've laid eyes on you," he says, flicking his hair back with his hand for effect and flashing his teeth in a wide smile that looks like he's trying out for a toothpaste commercial.

At which point I can't contain a really loud snort and start cracking up, which apparently is not the response he's expecting.

"Fine, be that way," he growls before calling me something not very nice. He stomps off and jaywalks across the street.

What way? I wonder. Is it my fault for laughing if he says something that sounds like a line out of a really corny romcom?

Whatever. I decide to keep my eyes on the sidewalk to avoid eye or smile contact until I get to our building. It feels safer that way.

Victor, the doorman, is standing under the awning doing what he loves best, watching diverse New Yorkers in their interesting fashion choices walk by. Ever since I was a little kid, I've loved hanging out with him and listening to his observations. He's always got Tootsie

Rolls in his pocket, and he's not afraid to share them.

"Hi, Victor," I say, grateful to have made it home without any more random weirdness.

"Good a-fternoon?" he replies, looking at me curiously, as if trying to figure out who I am.

What? This guy has known me since the day my parents brought me home from the hospital.

"Victor, it's *me*, Rosie! *Rosie Charming*."

The look of recognition as it dawns on his mustachioed face is almost comical.

"Goodness gracious, Miss Rosie, I didn't recognize you all dressed up like that! You look . . . quite the young lady."

"Yeah, it's a little different, isn't it?" I say, trying to dispel the awkwardness. "Mom thought I needed a bit of 'styling.'"

I do air quotes with my fingers, because I don't want him to think I'm taking this whole makeover thing too seriously.

"But I'm still the same old me," I assure him.

"Of course you are, Miss Rosie," he says. "You look lovely."

He reaches into his pocket as if he's going to offer me a Tootsie Roll like he usually does, then stops and shakes his head.

"I suppose you're too sophisticated to want a Tootsie Roll now, Miss Rosie."

He sounds sad.

"No way!" I tell him. "I'll never be too old or sophisticated for that."

Victor smiles and hands me a piece of candy, just like always. It's comforting after all the strange stuff that's been happening since I left the department store.

"Thanks, Victor. See you tomorrow!"

I head to the elevator, but when I glance back, he's staring at me, shaking his head, like he still can't believe I'm the same kid he's known since she was a baby.

My reflection freaks me out when the door opens and I see her looking at me from the reflective glass in the elevator. I quickly turn my back, press the button for our floor, and stare fixedly at the elevator door, willing it to open so I can get out and away from Mirror Girl.

Fairest in the Land . . .

No. Stop it. *Lalalalalalalala!* I can't hear you! *Lalalalalalalalala!*

I escape as soon as the door opens, and let myself into the apartment. I can hear Mom and Dad in the living room.

"Hi, I'm home!" I call out.

"Rosie, come!" Mom orders, like I'm a puppy in obedience school. "Let's see the results of Phillipe's magic."

I drop my bags outside the kitchen, take a deep breath, and walk into the living room.

Not even the rush hour smiles and being chatted up by a random boy on the street have prepared me for Dad's reaction.

"Rosamunde White Charming! What have you done to yourself?"

He looks like a disapproving school principal, and not just because his reading glasses are perched on the end of his nose. Yes, ladies, sorry to disappoint you, but it's true. He had to get them when he hit forty. Even Prince Charming isn't immune to the ravages of age and time.

"Relax, Ivan," Mom says, putting her hand on his arm and petting him like he's an overwrought sheepdog. "She looks beautiful. Who needs a fairy godmother when Charming Lifestyles offers Phillipe."

She gets that "aha!" look that's all too familiar.

"That would be a great tagline. Where's my pad and pen?"

"Just use the voice memo on your phone, Mom," I tell her. "That's what it's for."

"Good idea," she says.

Of course it takes her almost as long to figure out where the voice memo app is located, how to use it, and to repeat her moment of inspiration as it would for me to go to the kitchen and get her a pen and paper. And in the meantime I'm standing there like a Très Cher store mannequin while Dad regards me in awkward silence.

When Mom finishes recording herself, she surveys me again.

"Maybe we should put before and after shots of you on the website. It would be a great advertisement for Phillipe's work."

"NO WAY!" I shout.

"OVER MY DEAD BODY!" Dad shouts at the same time.

At least we agree on *something*.

Mom stares at us like we've gone insane.

"What's the matter with you two?" she inquires, her voice taking on that deceptive sweetness that covers up a will of tempered steel.

"No way are we putting pictures of Rosie looking like that on the website," Dad says.

"Looking like *what*?" Mom says. "Are you saying she isn't beautiful?"

Hello, parents? I'm standing right here!

Dad glances at me and gives me a weak smile.

"Darling, you look lovely. Really. Absolutely, totally breathtaking." He sounds sincere enough when he says it. But then he adds, "It's just . . ."

And I want to crawl under a rock. It's just *what*?

"It's just that your father can't handle the fact that his little girl is growing up," Mom says, her voice tinged with irritation. "He wants you to stay a tomboy. He'd be happy if you never had a date, ever."

"That's not fair!" Dad says.

"Isn't it?" Mom asks, her midnight dark eyebrow arched questioningly. "So what, exactly, is the problem here?"

"I . . . I . . . ," Dad sputters.

"I'm going to my room," I tell them. "Let me know when the fight is over."

"We're not fighting, Rosie dear, we're *discussing*," Mom says.

"Whatever. Just call me when it's time for dinner."

I grab my backpack and the shopping bag and head to my room. Luckily, Nicole and Katie are online, so I get them on group video chat.

"Wait. . . . Is that really you?" Nicole says. "Rosie Charming?"

"Yeah, it's me," I sigh.

"*Wowza!*" Katie exclaims. "You look so . . . different!"

"*Good* different or *bad* different?"

"Amazing," Nicole says.

"Totally," Katie agrees. "I can't believe your hair. And that outfit is adorable."

"There's more where that came from," I say, holding up the shopping bag.

"Let's see!" Katie squeals.

Luckily for me, the Minions packed each outfit wrapped in tissue, so I don't have the embarrassment of having to whip out my phone to check the pictures to make sure I've got the right components.

"Love. It." Nicole says.

"Me too!" Katie agrees.

They like the next three just as much.

"I can't believe your parents bought you all those clothes at once," Katie sighs as I hold up the last outfit from the bag. "It's like a dream come true."

I decide to keep quiet about all the other outfits that are being sent.

"I know, right?" Nicole says. "And from Très Cher too. I can't even imagine how much that must have all cost."

"Mom gets a special discount," I say, not even knowing if that's true. "You guys can borrow stuff."

Katie smiles.

"I call first dibs on the flowery skirt," she says. "It's so pretty."

"Do you guys . . ." I hesitate, afraid to voice what's bothering me.

"What?" Nicole asks.

"Do I still look like me?" I ask. "I mean, do you think it's okay, this whole makeover business?"

"You look great!" Katie says. "You look like you, but more . . . I don't know . . . sophisticated. Polished. Like you could be in a magazine. Like you'd stand out in a crowd."

That's exactly what I'm afraid of. . . .

"How do *you* feel about it?" Nicole asks.

I've been fidgeting with the jeweled compact Mom gave me, and now I open it to look at myself.

Fairest in the Land . . . Own it.

"I don't know," I say, suddenly feelingly myself drawn to the reflection of New Me like a bear to honey.

"Well, as long as you're happy, that's all that matters," Nicole says.

You are the one that matters, Fairest in the Land.

"I have to go," I say, tearing my eyes away from New Me with difficulty to say good-bye to my friends. "I'll see you tomorrow."

I slam the compact shut and spend the rest of the night avoiding my reflection.

Dad apologizes to me again at breakfast the next morning. It's as awkward as it was the night before at dinner.

"Honey, I'm sorry again about yesterday when you came home. I didn't mean to make you feel . . ."

I'm more than willing to fill in the blanks for him.

"Uncomfortable? Like an idiot? Dorky?"

Dad flushes. Mom gives him an *I told you so* smirk.

"Any of those things." He sighs and takes my hand. "I guess Mom's right, like she always is. . . . Well, except when it comes to Stranger Danger. I'm not ready for my little princess to grow up."

I love my dad, but it's *waaaaay* too early for him to be this sappy. I pull my hand away.

"Sheesh, Dad, it's not like I'm getting married. I just want a date for the Fall Festive."

"The kids at your school have to be idiots if they don't ask you," Dad says. "Right, Snow?"

But Mom's busy making her first filtered spring water biome organic fruit and kelp smoothie of the day. She alternates between kelp and wood betony.

A mixture of land and sea keeps you holistically balanced, just like Mother Nature intended! claimed the article she wrote about it on CharmingLifestyles.com, *complete with delicious smoothie recipes!*

I've tasted her health shakes, and personally, I'd rather go for a slice of pizza and being imbalanced any day.

As I sit down I catch a glimpse of myself reflected in the polished chrome of the toaster. I've never noticed my reflection so often before.

That's because you weren't as much to look at.

"Mom, can I have some of your smoothie?" I hear myself saying.

Dad lays his coffee cup warmed fingers across my forehead.

"Are you feeling okay, Rosie? You hate that stuff!"

He leans back and picks up his mug again, grinning. "Did Phillipe color your thoughts as well as your hair?"

I'm starting to wonder that myself.

Chapter Five

I PICK UP AN APPLE TO SUPPLEMENT MY
lunch at the fruit stand near the bus stop. We're not
allowed to have apples in the house, because Mom developed a severe aversion to them after the Not Quite Dead
incident—even if it did lead to her meeting Dad and living happily ever after.

It's too bad, because both Dad and I love apples, especially apple pie with vanilla ice cream. Sometimes we
sneak out to the coffee shop on East Seventy-Ninth Street
for a pie à la mode fix. The waitresses get all giggly over
Dad, which is super annoying, but the fact that they give
us extra big slices almost makes up for it.

You'd think Mom would be allergic to anything that resembles a stay or a girdle too, after Stepgrandmother tried to kill her with one of those, but instead she managed to transform *that* particular posttraumatic stress into her very profitable line of StaySvelte™ bodyshapers.

Even though I don't get a seat on the bus, I take out my *Romeo and Juliet* essay to reread it one last time before handing it in. Mrs. Minnich is probably expecting me to write about the romance because of my parents, not understanding that it's *because* of my parents I think Romeo and Juliet are insane. Maybe I just should have faked an appreciation of true love so I could get an A.

Oh well, too late now. I sigh and try to stuff the paper back into my backpack without mangling it, which isn't easy in a crowded bus at rush hour, let me tell you.

The bus stops on the corner of the block where the Manhattan World Themes Middle School is located. Students crowd the sidewalk, treasuring their last few minutes of freedom before school starts.

Hunter Farthington, Katie's date candidate, is standing right near the bus stop with a bunch of his soccer teammates, one of whom is Quinn Fairchild, Katie's new boyfriend. Just in case anyone might have missed that

Hunter's on the soccer team, he's wearing a MWTMS Soccer sweatshirt, has a New York Red Bulls sports bag over his shoulder, and he's attempting to spin a soccer ball on his finger.

"Hey, Hunter," I say as I walk by.

The ball drops from his finger and rolls toward the street as he looks at me, his mouth open. I get to the ball before it reaches the curb and kick it back to him, which hurts my foot more than it normally would because I'm wearing ballet flats instead of my usual Converse.

Thing that Mom never writes about on CharmingLifestyles.com but should: Putting your best fashion foot forward can be painful!

"Uh . . . thanks," Hunter says. He continues staring as I pass by. The guy is cute, but the gawping expression he's sporting isn't his best look.

I spot Katie and Nicole and make a beeline for them. Nicole wolf-whistles.

"Well, look at you, Miss Rosie Charming!"

"Come on, give us a twirl," Katie says.

"Do I have to?" I groan. "People are already looking."

"Yes, you do," Katie orders, and I give a reluctant spin.

"Isn't getting people to look the point of looking good?" Nicole asks.

"Is it?" I mean, I know Mom always writes about

putting your best self forward in her CharmingLifestyles.com pieces, but is that just so people will look at you?

"You know what I mean," Nicole says.

I smile and shrug, but I'm not sure I do.

"Yeah, Hunter Farthington actually took his eyes off the soccer ball when you walked by," Katie crowed. "He's totally going to ask you to the Fall Festive. I know it."

"Well, I bet Damien Wolfe will stop drawing comics for a minute when Rosie walks into Language Arts, and he'll ask her first," Nicole huffs.

"How much do you want to bet?" Katie says.

"Um . . . guys? I'm standing right here!" I remind them.

My presence apparently doesn't seem to affect their eagerness to wager on my dating prospects.

"I'll bet you a CandyFloss Lipgloss that Damien asks her first," Nicole says.

"Done!" Katie agrees. They fist-bump to seal the wager.

"Now that you've bet on me like I'm a racehorse, can I get some advice?" I say.

They finally appear to remember I'm there and a real person, not just a dating project.

"Sorry, Rosie!" Katie says, hugging me.

"Me too," Nicole agrees. "I guess we got a little carried away."

I think of how I actually asked my mom for some of her kelp and betony smoothie this morning—*Note to self: It tasted just as disgusting as last time*—and tell them, "No problem. It's easy to do."

"So, how can we help?" Katie asks.

"I'm not sure, exactly. I just . . . well, flirting isn't my thing, if you know what I mean. And I tried googling *How to get a date in middle school* and—"

"Wait . . . You *googled* how to get a date in middle school?" Nicole asks.

"Uh . . . yeah," I confess.

"For reals?" Katie says, barely able to contain her laughter.

I nod.

The two of them start cracking up. They practically have to hold each other up because they're laughing so hard.

"What did it *say*?!" Nicole asks.

"That's the problem," I tell them. "It was all this conflicting advice that totally confused me, like: *Be charming and funny—but not too flirtatious* . . . and *be confident, but don't come across as loud and strident*. I mean, seriously. How are you supposed to know if you're doing that?"

"Because we're here to tell you," Katie says.

"Yeah, don't worry, we'll keep you in line," Nicole assures me.

Katie lets go another snort of laughter. "I still can't believe you asked Google for dating advice instead of us."

"I still can't believe I asked *my mother* for dating advice," I mutter.

"Hey, look at all the amazing clothes you scored," Nicole points out. "I'd ask my mom for advice in a second if it meant a shopping spree at Très Cher."

Just like that, I feel like an ungrateful brat. I *am* lucky that my mom was willing to do so much for me. I just wish it didn't all feel so strange and . . . uncomfortable.

"You're right," I say. "I'm sure this will all work out and I'll have a date for the dance in no time. Maybe even by the end of today if I'm lucky."

"That's right," Katie says. "Positive attitude."

If only I actually believed the words coming out of my mouth.

Damien Wolfe, Nicole's dance date candidate, is in my first period math class. So is Nicole, and she spends the entire time we're walking to class telling me his eyes are going to pop out of his head when he sees the new, improved Rosie. I find this hard to believe.

Sure enough, when we walk into the classroom, Damien is in his usual seat in the back, sketching in his notebook, and his eyes remain firmly in his head. In fact, he doesn't even notice that we've entered the room.

Why not?

Well, he *is* busy drawing, as usual. I find myself strangely miffed that even Mirror Girl isn't enough to draw his attention. It feels like a challenge—one that I'm determined to win.

So I "accidentally" drop my books right near his foot—except one of them, the really heavy math text-book, lands *on* his foot, and he jumps up with an excla-mation of pain. That part really *was* an accident. Cross my heart, I do not lie.

"Omigosh, I'm *so* sorry, Damien!" I exclaim. "Are you okay?"

He sits back down, holding his toe through his sneaker, as I pick up my books.

"I'll live," he says. "But can you call AAA? I think I might need a toe truck."

A tow truck?

"Oh!" I giggle, finally getting it. "Sure. I have them on speed dial."

"Why, do you make a habit of dropping heavy books on people's toes?" he asks.

"No, I . . . Never mind," I mumble, turning to go to my desk.

This definitely isn't going the way I thought it would.

"Nice haircut," Damien says just as I sit down, convinced the whole thing has been a complete fail.

I smile my thanks back at him as class begins, feeling a warm glow of . . . *victory.*

Hunter Farthington is in my PE class, which is next. We're doing a unit on yoga, which is supposed to help us learn how to de-stress and be mindful, except inevitably someone farts and everyone cracks up. Then Coach W gets mad and starts *not yelling* in her *I'm not going to shout because this is yoga but if it weren't I'd totally be screaming at you* voice, which makes it even more stressful than dodgeball. There's something about her carefully suppressed fury that's scarier than when Coach G, the other PE teacher, shouts at the top of his lungs across the gym.

"So, what prompted this sudden makeover?" Genny Krulinski asks when we're getting changed in the locker room.

"I don't know—I guess I just felt like a change," I lie.

I'm not about to admit to Genny Krulinski that I was willing to try pretty much anything to get a date for the Fall Festive—including asking my mother for advice.

"Pretty radical change," Genny says.

"Really?" I respond as casually as I can manage. "You think so?"

She gives me a "duh" look.

"One day you're the Thrift Store Queen and the next day you're a walking ad for Très Cher. I'd say that's pretty radical."

"Well, I think you look pretty, period," Aria Thornebriar says. "What's the matter with changing it up once in a while?"

"I didn't *say* there was anything the matter," Genny huffs, taking her towel and stomping away, even though the way she said it made it sound like there was.

"Don't let Genny get to you," Aria says. "I think she's just jealous because of how Hunter reacted this morning. She's had a crush on him since sixth grade."

"What do you mean?" I ask as we walk out to the gym together.

Aria gives me a skeptical look.

"Oh, come on. Tell me you didn't notice how he could barely string together a sentence when you showed up this morning?" she says.

"Well . . ."

"Okay, I know Hunter isn't a great conversationalist at the best of times, but it was even worse."

I know it's wrong, but I can't help laughing.

"Yes, I noticed," I admit.

"Well, so did Genny Krulinski. And if looks could kill, you'd be lying in a glass coffin like your mom," Aria says.

I'm taken aback that she brings up Mom and The Tale so casually, like it's no biggie. Nobody at school ever talks about it, even though they know. I think it's a New York City thing. So many celebrities live here that it's uncool to be starstruck. But I guess Aria knows what it's like to be the daughter of celebrity parents. Her mom is Briar Rose, aka Sleeping Beauty.

"Well, luckily for me, I'm still alive and kicking," I joke, heading to get a yoga mat. "Now I just have to try and get through yoga without dying."

"Or even worse, farting," Aria says.

"Why does everyone fart during yoga?" I ask. "It's like an epidemic."

"No, it's natural," Aria explains. "I googled *Why does*

yoga make you fart and got over four hundred and sixty thousand results."

Note to Katie and Nicole: I'm not the only person at Manhattan World Themes Middle School who googles weird things.

Genny's mat is right next to Hunter's. She's asking him about yesterday's practice like it's the most interesting thing on earth.

Did she google How to get a date in middle school *too, I wonder?*

I can't help feeling satisfaction when Genny lets an enormous booty bomb go when we're doing the plow pose, and the entire class starts cracking up, Hunter and his friends loudest of all.

Or when Hunter smiles up at me as I look at him upside down while doing the downward dog.

Fairest in the Land . . . Own it.

Smiles are a good first step, but I still need him to go further than that. I need him—or Damien—to ask me to the dance.

Chapter Six

I DECIDE THAT IT'S TIME FOR ADVICE THAT isn't Mom, or Dad, or my friends. I need some insight on guys from some real, live guys. Luckily, I know just the place to get that because I know seven who live all together in one apartment. Mom used to do housework for them, once upon a time.

My seven height disadvantaged "uncles" used to live across the Seven Mountains. Now they live across Central Park on West Seventy-Seventh. If I were wearing my Converse I'd walk through the park, but after just one day at school these ballet flats are already giving me a blister, so I take the crosstown bus instead.

My uncles would never take the bus—they prefer being underground. That's one of the reasons they insisted on buying a basement apartment on West Seventy-Seventh—so they'd have the double benefits of as little sunlight as possible and being near the subway.

These days they're not swinging their pickaxes to mine precious gems. Instead, they work in more comfortable surroundings in the diamond district, dealing in stones and fashion jewelry for CharmingLifestyles.com. Mom and Dad (and CynCorp) get a percentage of the sale in exchange for merchandising the gems, and everybody's happy.

Everyone's happy except for Uncle Herb, that is. Dad says Herb's not happy unless he's unhappy. This doesn't make the slightest sense to me, because he seems to be unhappy all the time, which means he should be happy, right? Grown-up logic can be so twisted.

When I get to their building, I go down the steps to their door, which is below street level. It's the kind of apartment that most people wouldn't think is that desirable because of security and lack of light, but my uncles were willing to pay a premium for it. Getting seven short cohabiting bachelors past the co-op board wasn't easy, but when Snow White and Prince Charming showed up to give them all personal character references, it sealed the deal. Celebrity has its privileges.

Uncle Shrimpy answers the door. He's the one a lot of people think is stupid, but Mom says he just thinks differently from the way most people do. That's for sure. Today his hair is dyed bright purple and he's wearing red velvet shorts, a black T-shirt with a glittery gold star on it, and a pair of three-inch gold platform shoes.

"Rosie honey!" he exclaims, wrapping me in a hug, which is always awkward, because even in three-inch platforms his face comes up to my belly button.

"What's up, Uncle Shrimpy?" I ask. "*Love* the outfit."

"This old thing?" he says, with a dismissive wave. "But aren't these shoes great? I got them at the thrift store on Ninety-Seventh."

Uncle Shrimpy knows all the best thrift stores. Everything I know about getting good deals on vintage clothes I learned from him.

"Totally awesome," I tell him. "Just make sure you don't break your ankle."

"Hey, guys, our little Rosie's here!" Shrimpy shouts.

Considering that I've towered over all of them since I was eight, it's both funny and comforting that my uncles still consider me their "little Rosie." I follow Uncle Shrimpy into the living room, where Uncles Jem, Zafiro,

Yù, and Bijou are hanging out on their child-sized chairs and sofas. They keep two full-sized chairs for when Mom and Dad come to visit, and deciding that my new outfit makes me more grown-up, I sit on one of them, instead of in my usual kiddie chair.

The act does not escape Uncle Jem's notice. Very little does.

"Does the sophisticated new outfit and your decision to perch your bottom on your mother's chair signal that you have acquired ambitions of a more . . . shall we say . . . rebellious adolescent nature?"

If he hadn't been born with a height disadvantage in the days before there were laws against discrimination, Uncle Jem could have been a diplomat.

"No, no, no." Uncle Zafiro shakes his head and surveys me with disapproving dark eyes. "This is trouble. This is about the boys. I feel it in my bones. *Trouble*, I tell you."

"Zaffy, man, the only thing you feel in your bones is arthritis," argues Uncle Bijou. "Our Rosie is just learning to shine like the star she's meant to be."

He beams at me, his teeth gleaming white against the darkness of his skin.

I smile at Uncle Bijou, even though I know that Uncle Zafiro is the one who is right.

"Are you *nuts? NO MORE GARLIC!*"

Uh-oh. It sounds like Uncle Herb is getting into another argument with Uncle Rocco in the kitchen. They are both *extremely* passionate about food. Against my better judgment, I decide to play peacemaker and get up to go see what's happening.

Uncle Rocco looks like a knight with a saber, waving a chef's knife that's almost as long as his arm, except instead of armor he's wearing a tomato sauce spattered apron. At least I'm pretty sure it's tomato, because I don't see any blood on Uncle Herb. *Yet.*

"*YOU* are the crazy one!" Uncle Rocco spits, with a dangerous swish of the knife. "It needs more garlic, not to mention black pepper!"

Uncle Herb appears to be defending himself with a large wooden spoon that is dripping globs of sauce all over the floor.

"It looks like a police show crime scene in here," I observe. "But it *smells* delicious."

They finally stop glaring at each other long enough to notice I'm standing there, and seriously, it's like someone waved a magic wand—and fortunately, not one covered with tomato sauce—because Uncle Rocco's stony expression turns to a broad smile underneath his graying mustache, and Uncle Herb grins and puts the wooden spoon back into the huge pot that's bubbling on the stove.

"Look at our little princess," Uncle Herb says, moving to hug me. "Doesn't she look a pretty picture?"

"Um, maybe you could wipe off the tomato sauce before you hug me?" I suggest, sidestepping his embrace. "This is a brand-new outfit."

Uncle Rocco, who was coming in for the embrace too, takes a step back along with Herb, and they both blush to match their aprons.

"Sorry, Rosie," Rocco mumbles, surveying the state of Herb, the kitchen, and himself. "I guess we got a little carried away."

"Well, he did, anyway," Herb mutters. "With the garlic."

"Only because you put in too much basil and—"

"Okay, *time-out!*" I say, making a T with my hands. "Gentlemen, to your corners."

To my confusion, they look at each other and burst out laughing—and I'm talking some serious guffaws. Uncle Rocco throws his arm around Uncle Herb, who is wiping tears of laughter from his eyes, as if they weren't just threatening each other with kitchen tools only moments before.

"What?" I ask. "What's so funny?"

"You remind me more of your mother every day," Uncle Rocco gasps.

"She's even starting to look more like Snow," Herb adds.

Between them and the Mirror going on and on about that Fairest in the Land stuff, I'm starting to feel like I'm reliving a creepy version of The Tale.

"If you've finished trying to murder each other, can you come sit down with the rest of the uncles?" I say. "I need your advice."

"Advice?" Uncle Herb's face lights up, and he takes off his apron. "You've come to the right place. We gave your mother lots of good advice."

"Yeah," Uncle Rocco says. "Too bad she didn't listen to any of it."

"I'm not my mother," I snap. "I know all about Stranger Danger."

I can hear crazy rhymes coming from where I dropped my backpack on the living room floor: *Pay no heed to the men of no height; you're the one who is beautiful, and right.*

Call me crazy, but I'm really starting to believe the Mirror in that compact Mom gave me talks just like *the* Mirror.

"I bet you say that to all the girls," I mutter.

"Say what to all the girls?" Uncle Herb asks.

"Yeah, it's not like Herb is such a . . . what do they call them these days . . . a chick magnet?" Uncle Rocco says, washing off his hands and face.

"And you are?" Herb retorts. "You haven't been on a date since . . . what? . . . 1784?"

Rocco turns from the sink, dripping wet hands outstretched like he's about to put them around Herb's neck.

"*O-kay*, about that advice," I remind them, hoping to head off another fight.

Rocco lowers his hands and wipes them dry on a non-tomatoey dish towel.

"C'mon, Herb. Rosie needs our wisdom."

Uncle Jem winks at me as I lead the two warring uncles back into the living room.

"Nice work," he mouths.

Once we're all seated, I take a deep breath and start explaining the problem.

"So, there's this dance coming up at school a week from Saturday called the Fall Festive—"

"See!" Zafiro interrupts, pumping his fist in triumph. "I knew this was about boy trouble." He taps the side of his nose. "Zafiro's nose never fails to sniff out the truth!"

"Maybe because Zafiro's nose takes up most of his face," Bijou says.

I'm starting to wonder if this whole *asking the uncles for advice* idea was a mistake, but since I've already taken the bus across town *and* broken up a fight, I might as well go for it.

"It's not exactly boy trouble, Uncle Zafiro. It's *lack of boy* trouble," I explain. "I still don't have a date. That's why Mom thought I needed some fashion guidance, so she sent me to Phillipe for a consultation. And that's why I look like this."

"*This* happens to be very lovely," Uncle Jem observes.

"Yeah, I guess," I say, not willing to admit that I'm both disturbed by Mirror Girl yet aware she has certain perks; or that I've started hearing the strange voice from the compact in my bag, which has now gone quiet again. "But I still don't have a date. So, I need advice on how to find one. And you are the only guys I know that I can ask such an embarrassing question."

They all smile. Uncle Shrimpy actually takes out a large white hanky from the pocket of his tiny red velvet shorts and starts dabbing his eyes, he's so overcome by emotion.

"It's my considered opinion that any young man who *doesn't* want to go out with you needs his head examined at the earliest opportunity," says Uncle Jem.

It's really nice to hear him say that but . . .

"You have to say that because you're my uncle," I say.

"Well, technically I'm not really your uncle," Jem points out. "It's an honorific your mother bestowed on us when you were born."

"Minor detail," I say. "You're still not about to come out and tell me that I'm the last girl on earth that any guy would want to ask to the Fall Festive."

"You want some advice, Rosie? The way to a man's heart is through his stomach," Uncle Herb tells me. "Bring a nice pastrami sandwich on rye with mayo and mustard and maybe a little bit of lettuce—but not too much. Oh, and a sour deli pickle. That'll do it."

"Food's okay, but *music* is the soul of love," Uncle Bijou argues. "Find out what rocks his soul and walk by singing that song."

"But I have the worst singing voice in the history of ever," I say. "When we go to karaoke, nobody even wants me as a backup singer!"

"Minor detail," Bijou says, waving away my concern.

"Hang out at the gym," Rocco advises me. "Talk to a nice strong guy with good muscles. Someone who can protect you."

The other uncles nod. They clearly think I've inherited

Mom's obliviousness to Stranger Danger. *Hello, Uncles? This girl was born and raised in New York City!*

"So, I should sing while bringing a pastrami sandwich to a nice muscular guy at the gym?"

"Not all three at the same time," Uncle Yù advises, stroking his goatee. "That could get messy."

"While you're singing, you should dance," Uncle Zafiro says. "Dancing reveals a woman's soul fire."

Um . . . what? I'm not exactly sure what my soul fire is, but I'm pretty sure I don't want it revealed. At this point I'm starting to wonder if I want to go to this stupid dance at all.

You cannot stop your quest so grand
To be the Fairest in the Land.
Fear not, be ruthless, and yes, be strong
And do not leave the road you're on.

I know that mirror is a precious ancient family heirloom, but at this point I'm starting to wish it came with a mute button. Why didn't Mom warn me that it liked to chatter?

My uncles are still doling out the advice like it's candy on Halloween.

"Don't eat beans," Uncle Jem says. "Flatulence isn't flattering."

"Okay, no beans," I repeat.

"Or garlic," Uncle Herb says, studiously ignoring Uncle Rocco, whose face immediately flushes red with fury.

No way am I going to let them start the Garlic War up again. Not when I'm getting important dating advice.

"Please, Uncs," I plead. "Don't fight. I really need your help."

"That's right, Herb," Rocco says, all holier-than-thou. "Rosie needs us."

Uncle Herb harrumphs and crosses his arms across his chest.

"I will examine the charts to determine the most auspicious day for Rosie's dating quest," Uncle Yù says, getting up and going over to his desk, which is cluttered with parchments and a seriously vintage quill pen.

"But, Uncle Yù, the dance is a week from Saturday," I point out. "I don't have time to wait for auspicious days. I already feel like a loser for not having a date yet. Especially because I'm You Know Who's daughter."

Snow White is fair, it's true to say,

But your youth can beat her any day.

Did Mom's mirror just *diss* her? Burn.

Still, I can't help feeling a small thrill that there's someone in this world—or rather some*thing*—that thinks I'm fairer than my mother, whose beauty is the stuff of legend.

"I am aware of the date," Uncle Yù says, putting on his glasses and bending over one of his parchments. "Remember, Rosie: Patience, and the mulberry leaf becomes a silk gown."

Uncle Yù is full of proverbs that sound totally profound, but I'm never really sure exactly what they mean.

My head is starting to spin from all my uncles telling me to do different things, and the Mirror's mutterings. I close my eyes, wondering why I have to have a date for the dance anyway. Maybe I could just go by myself and then run away at midnight, leaving one of my shoes on the steps or something.

But that's someone else's tale.

The only uncle who hasn't given me any advice is Shrimpy. He's just been listening and watching, his big blue eyes taking everything in like they always do, as he paints his nails purple to match his hair.

"What about you, Shrimpy?" I ask. "Do you have any words of wisdom?"

He blows on the nails of his left hand and waves it gently to dry them.

"I think you should just be yourself," he says. "Because

Rosie Charming is the best thing you can be."

Yeah. Like that's worked so well to date.

As I take the crosstown bus home, I wonder if getting dating advice from my uncles, who to my knowledge haven't done that much dating, was a good idea. But dateless Charmings can't be choosy. I need all the help I can get.

Chapter Seven

I STOP AT THE GROCERY STORE ON THE way home, trying to figure out what I should make as date bait. Pastrami sandwiches are too smelly to carry around in school all day, and besides, I think you have to keep them cold. I haven't read this in any of Mom's CharmingLifestyles.com articles, but I'm pretty sure that giving a guy food poisoning would be major dating no-no.

There's always the Shiny Red Apple trick, I muse as I walk through the produce section, but somehow I don't see guys at a New York City school falling for that as easily as Mom did.

I figure cookies are my best bet. They're small, portable, and don't need to be refrigerated. Plus, they smell *waaaaaay* better than pastrami. Now the question is: If the quickest way to a man's heart is through his stomach, would it be cheating to use a mix instead of baking them from scratch? The Need-a-Date clock is ticking.

If I were a CharmingLifestyles.com reader, I'd put on a cute little apron and whip up five different types of cookies, while weaving, then decorating the cute little baskets to present them in, all without chipping my nail polish or breaking a sweat. Or at least that's what Mom's breezy articles imply. She always looks cool as a cucumber in the how-to videos and pictures.

But I know what *really* happens at those photo shoots. Mom has one assistant doing the shopping, another doing prep, and a third doing most of the baking. She walks in to do a few stirs of the bowl and has the makeup artist blotting her face and applying powder so Mom is able to maintain a dewy, flawless complexion no matter how hot it gets in the kitchen.

I decide to go for the cookie mix, since *I'm* baking solo and have homework to do besides.

"Let me help you with the bag," Victor says when I get to our building.

"Thanks, Victor," I say, handing it to him gratefully. Being bombarded with dating advice has really taken it out of me.

"You look tuckered out," he says, reaching into his jacket and pulling out a Tootsie Roll. "You need a pre-homework treat."

I'm reaching for the Tootsie Roll when I hear the Mirror's voice from my backpack:

Think again before you eat

This aging servant's common treat.

A momentary pleasure taste

Another inch grows on your waist.

Pulling my hand back to my side, I say, "No thanks, too fattening."

Victor's face falls. "Oh. Okay. I guess young ladies have to watch their figures," he says.

The elevator opens and he hands me the shopping bag.

"You look terrific, as far as I'm concerned, Miss Rosie," Victor calls out as the door closes.

But all I can hear in my head is the Mirror's voice.

Mom is in the kitchen making a cup of rose hip and cinnamon tea (*Great for the complexion! On sale now for $8.99 at CharmingLifestyles.com*).

"How was your day, Rosie?" she asks.

"Okay, I guess. The uncs send their love."

"Are Herb and Rocco still bickering?" Mom asks.

"'Bickering' would be an understatement. They were both covered in tomato sauce and the kitchen looked like a *Law and Order* crime scene."

Mom laughs.

"That's the real reason I took over the cooking. It was the only way to get any peace and quiet."

"You mean it wasn't really for room and board?"

"I did the cleaning and laundry for room and board. Herb and Rocco didn't actually want to give up the cooking. They enjoy it."

"Yeah, I think they like fighting, too."

Mom nods and takes a sip of tea.

"The two of them are never as happy as when they're throwing sauce at each other in the middle of an argument. I just got sick of having to wash all the extra dishrags. No such thing as paper towels in the woods beyond the Seven Mountains."

"I know, and I don't know how lucky I am to be growing up in New York City with so many modern conveniences," I sigh. I've heard that speech so many times I could give it myself.

"Okay, SassyPants. I'm going back to work," Mom says.

"Have fun making lives more Charming!" I tell her. But as she is about to leave the kitchen, I call out, "Wait. Mom?"

"What, dear?"

"You know the Mirror you gave me? The family heirloom thing?"

"Yes. What about it?"

"Did . . . I mean . . . Did you ever hear it *say anything*?"

"As in *talk*?"

I nod, hoping she doesn't reach for the phone to call an ambulance to take me away.

But instead she laughs.

"Rosie dear, I think you're getting much too stressed out about finding a date if you're starting to hear things," she says. "Let me make you a cup of soothing chamomile and lemon balm tea."

"No, it's okay," I say. "I was probably just imagining it. You know, because I've heard The Tale so many times."

Mom comes and cups my cheek with her long, white fingers.

"Are you sure you're okay?" she asks.

"Yeah. I'm fine," I say, shrugging. "I just have cookies to bake and homework to do—that's all."

She looks into my eyes, as if searching for the truth. I turn away, not wanting her to see that I'm lying. Because I'm not just imagining it—the Mirror definitely speaks.

"Okay. If you're sure," Mom says finally. "I've got another listicle to write before dinner."

I make the cookies according to the instruction on the box. Once they're cooling on the rack, I take out my books to do my homework. The compact slides out of my backpack onto the kitchen table with a heavy thunk. That thing really is solid gold. As sick as I am of hearing it talk to me all day, I can't help myself from opening it and looking at my reflection.

Rosamunde Charming, Princess Fair
Or would be if she combed her hair.

I snap it shut and shove it to the bottom of my backpack. Algebra homework is more fun than being dissed by a piece of talking glass.

Damien Wolfe is sitting at his usual desk in the back of math class the next morning, drawing something in his notebook with a thin black pen. When I get closer, I see that it's a comic strip.

"Hey, Damien," I say, holding out the small Ziploc bag of cookies, which I've decorated with colored Sharpies. It's not going to win me any prizes for presentation on the Food Channel, but I had homework to do. Getting a date for the dance is important, but so is making honor roll.

Damien looks startled, like a deer confronted by a predator in the woods. Meanwhile, I'm still holding the bag of cookies.

"These are for you," I say, pointing out the obvious.

Apparently, what is obvious to me is not as obvious to Damien.

"Uh, why?" he asks.

I can't tell the truth, which is that I'm trying to wangle my way into his heart with cookie goodness so he'll ask me to the dance. So I lie. Figuring that every day is a made-up greeting card holiday of some kind, I create one of my own.

"Well . . . it's Kookie Kindness Day," I lie. It sounds pretty lame, even to me.

He looks dubious, but takes the cookies and says, "Thanks. I never heard of that before."

"Yeah. It's one of those *paying it forward* things," I improvise. "You know, someone does something nice for you and then you do something nice for them."

"So, like, I should do something nice for someone else now?" Damien asks. "Because you gave me the cookies?"

I swear, this is the longest conversation we've ever had, and it's all based on me lying to him. But now that I've started this Kookie Kindness Day train, I can't seem to put the brakes on it.

Smiling brightly, I nod. "That's right. Pass it on. Pay it forward and all that."

Damien smiles, leaning back in his chair. He's really pretty cute when he smiles. He should do it more often.

"Cool," he says. "Thanks, Rosie."

One down, one to go.

"What was that all about?" Nicole whispers when I sit back at my desk.

I'm about to tell her that a way to a man's heart is through his stomach and how this is part of my *get a date to the dance* strategy, but Mr. Kostek is starting class.

"I'll tell you at lunch," I whisper.

I have PE right after this, and I have to run to get to the gym and get changed for yoga. Since Hunter is in my class, he can fulfill Uncle Rocco's *find a man with muscles* requirement.

Trying to figure out how to give Hunter a bag of cookies without embarrassing myself is totally messing with my mindfulness. The bag is stashed under my sweatshirt, which I've put under my towel next to my mat. When I'm supposed to be emptying my mind and concentrating on my "deep cleansing breaths," all I can think about are various methods of cookie transmission. I'm in the tree pose, trying hard not to lose my balance, when it finally comes to me. I'll just slide them to Hunter, who's right behind me, when we do the downward dog. Keep it simple, right?

Wrong.

When I go into downward dog, I reach over to grab the bag of cookies from under the sweatshirt so I can slide it over to Hunter. But I lose my balance and face-plant, painfully, onto my nose, which starts erupting bright red blood all over the yoga mat.

"Casualty! Man down!" Hunter shouts.

Clearly, he's been playing too many combat video games.

"I'm a *girl*, in case you didn't dotice," I manage to say from behind the towel I've bunged over my nose to try and contain the bleeding.

Genny Krulinski sniggers. No Kookie Kindness for her, that's for sure.

"Okay, stand back, everyone!" Coach W shouts. "No touching any bodily fluids!"

Great—she's acting like I have cooties or some highly

contagious flesh-eating disease that's going to contaminate everyone who comes into contact with my nose blood.

All calming breathing and meditation stops as Coach W goes to the first aid kit, dons plastic gloves and a face mask, and gets some paper towels and the spray bottle of industrial strength disinfectant that we use on the mats after class. She walks toward me, brandishing the disinfectant like she's about to spray me in the face, but at the last minute she barks: "Tip your head back and pinch your nose!" and sprays the mat down with enough liquid to kill any germs ten times over.

"What happened?" she asks.

"I uh . . . slipped."

"Well, take it easy. I don't want any injuries," Coach W says, stepping back from the mat, right onto my sweatshirt and the bag of cookies.

Too late for no injuries. And there goes my awesome plan for asking Hunter. I guess that's the way the cookie crumbles.

"That was a pretty spectacular nosedive," Aria says to me as I'm washing the blood from my face after class. "You look like you just came out of a boxing ring."

"I feel like it too," I say, touching my aching, tender

nose. "And Coach W stepped on the cookies I was going to give to Hunter Farthington for Kookie Kindness Day."

"What's Kookie Kindness Day?"

I explain the whole *paying it forward* thing.

"Why'd you pick Hunter?" she asks.

"What do you mean?"

"I don't know," Aria says, playing with the end of her braid. "I mean, Kookie Kindness is great and all, but he doesn't seem like your type." She shrugs. "Is that the point of it though? To reach out to people you wouldn't normally hang out with?"

"That's exactly right." Nodding my head hurts my nose. I hope it's not broken, although it would probably serve me right for being such a Pinocchio. "It's to try and make the world more friendly through cookies."

"Cool," Aria says as she heads to her locker to finish getting dressed. "I'm definitely going to do it."

I messed up at giving Hunter the cookies, lied to Damien and now Aria. Not only that, I've ended up with a really sore nose. This whole day is definitely *not* going according to plan.

"You'll never guess what happened!" Katie says when I meet her in the cafeteria. "Damien Wolfe gave Sophie McKee a black-and-white cookie in art. He said it was

Kookie Kindness Day, and he was paying it forward. Have you ever heard of anything so weird?"

I try to smile, but I'm having problems turning the corners of my mouth up because my brain is in panic mode and my nose hurts.

"Actually, I have. Someone was talking about it in first period."

I don't tell her that someone was yours truly.

"I never heard of it before," Katie says. "It's probably some stupid made-up holiday just to sell more greeting cards or something."

Well, she got the made-up part right.

And then Nicole joins us, and she's carrying one of those huge oatmeal raisin cookies they sell at the school café.

"Guys, look! Aria Thornebriar just gave me a cookie!" she exclaims. "She said it was for Kookie Kindness Day. I'm going to share it with you guys, because I'm paying it forward."

"How come no one has given *me* a cookie?" Katie complains. "Don't I deserve some Kookie Kindness? I'm starting to feel like a loser."

"Now you know how I feel when it comes to a date for the Fall Festive," I mutter.

Don't whine, Fair One, your prince will come
But not until your work is done.
Smooth hair, soft lips, and skin so clear.
Then surely will your date appear.

Is it possible to muzzle an inanimate object? Putting that on my Things to Google list.

"I'm sure you'll get a date by next Saturday," Nicole says in a sympathetic tone, which is easy for her, because she's already going with Dave Theis. "And, Katie, didn't I just say I'm sharing my Kookie Kindness with you?"

"I guess," Katie says. "But Quinn better give me a cookie, is all I can say."

"But this isn't supposed to be like Valentine's Day," I protest. "It's an act of kindness to a random person you're trying to reach out to, not to your significant other."

I can't believe I am making up new rules to the fake day that I made up this morning in first period. I am turning into Little Miss Liar McPantsonfire.

"Whatever," Katie grumbles, picking off another piece of oatmeal raisin cookie. "I still think he should give me one. Just because."

This whole thing is getting out of hand. What if Quinn doesn't give Katie a cookie, and she gets mad at him, and they break up and don't go to the dance? It would be all my fault for making up this stupid Kookie Kindness Day, because Damien Wolfe asked me why I was giving him cookies, and I didn't want to tell him the truth.

"Why don't *you* just give *him* one?" I ask. "Uncle Herb says the way to a man's heart is through his stomach."

Katie's face brightens.

"That's a great idea!" she says, getting two dollars out of her wallet. "I'm going to get him a chocolate chip cookie."

She goes off to the line to make her purchase, leaving Nicole and me to finish the cookie and eat our lunches.

"Katie might think it's stupid, but I love Kookie Kindness Day," Nicole says. "I was in a bad mood this morning, because my brother took so long in the shower that I couldn't wash my hair, and then I ripped my tights, because I was putting them on in such a hurry, and then I got a B minus on my science test and I thought I'd done better. . . ." She paused for a breath. "So when Aria Thornebriar handed me the cookie, just because it was Kookie Kindness Day, it turned my whole day around."

Huh. I can't really hate my stupid, made-up day if it's turned Nicole's day around like this, can I?

And as I walk through the hallways that afternoon, I notice that the atmosphere is different than it usually is. People are more animated, smiling at each other more, and kids who usually don't hang out are talking to one another.

Jenna Peasely gives a cookie to Mr. Scott, the janitor, and thanks him for keeping the school clean. This is Jenna Peasely, resident student body activist, who protests *everything* from the roughness of the toilet paper to the temperature of the water in the drinking fountains. I guess you can't blame her for being sensitive to things like that. When your mother is such a princess she can't sleep a wink all night and is black-and-blue because of one tiny pea placed under twenty mattresses, you're bound to end up with a few sensory issues.

When I walk past the office on the way out of school, Jackson Greenleaf, who spends half his life in there driving Mrs. Dickinson crazy, because he's always being sent to the principal for climbing things he shouldn't (his dad was the one who climbed the beanstalk, so I guess it's in the blood) is giving her a cookie. I feel like I'm walking through an alternative universe of happy, which is really cool—except that it was all started because I lied. Is it okay to feel less guilty about lying if it helped make the day better for others?

That's when I realize that Sophie McKee is walking

in front of me, talking to her friends. And that's when I overhear her say, "Then he asked me to the Fall Festive!"

My heart sinks. *Does she mean . . . ?*

"You're going to the Fall Festive with Damien Wolfe!" Sophie's friend exclaims. "Awesome!"

"I know, right?" Sophie says. "Kookie Kindness Day has turned out to be the best day ever!"

For everyone else, maybe. For me, not so much.

It's a week and two days till the Fall Festive, and I'm down to one date candidate, Hunter Farthington, the guy who thinks people from Ohio are called "Oheinies."

Luckily, I get a seat on the bus going home. I take the jeweled compact out of my backpack. Opening it, I see Mirror Girl reflected back at me.

I wonder if the Mirror answers questions, or if it only gives out unsolicited advice. It's worth a try.

Hey, Mirror, how come I can't get a date for the dance? I think.

At first I don't hear anything, and I wonder if now that I actually want to hear the Mirror's advice, it's finally stopped talking to me. But then it starts speaking up.

Princess Fair, if thou must ask
Then pray, perform this simple task.
Compose a poem, in proper form,
Not common speech as is the norm.

So, does that mean I have to think of a rhyme every time I want to ask the Mirror a question? Is the Mirror the ghost of a frustrated English teacher or something?

I rack my brain to think of a way to ask the question in verse. Poetry has never been one of my strengths.

Magic Mirror, I need a date
For my school dance before it's too late.
Tell me, Mirror, bring me joy.
How do I find my Fall Festive boy?

A few seconds later I hear the Mirror respond.

With shining hair and softest skin
Your reign as fairest will soon begin.
Stand straight, don't slouch, and then you'll see
The Fairest in the Land you'll be.

Let me get this straight. The Mirror's saying I don't have a date to the Fall Festive because I have *bad posture*?

I want to ask for clarification, but I'm too tired to make up another rhyme. Plus, there's a shifty-looking guy sitting in the seat across from me eyeing the jeweled compact in a way that's making me nervous. This *is* New York City, after all. I snap the compact shut and shove it to the bottom of my backpack for safety, hoping he gets off the bus before I do. Luckily, he does.

Whew! That was a major breach in city smarts. I'm

turning into Mom. *Stranger Danger, Rosie! Stranger Danger!*

When I get home, after I finish my homework, I practice walking up and down the hallway outside my room with a book on my head, just in case the Mirror is right and my dateless state *is* something to do with my slouching. It's just my luck that Dad happens to come home and catch me doing it.

"Is this some newfangled way of studying?" he asks, leaning against the wall with a huge grin on his face. "You walk around with the book on your head, expecting to absorb the knowledge by osmosis?"

I snatch the book off my head and scowl.

"No. I'm trying to improve my posture."

He pushes away from the wall and comes to kiss me on the forehead. "You know, you could just stand up straight instead of walking around with a book on your head."

"Wow, Dad. Why didn't I think of that?"

"What's brought on this sudden concern about posture, honey?" Dad asks. "Did something happen today?"

Part of me wants to tell Dad about how following the uncles' advice backfired on me today, and about the Mirror and what it said, but then I'm afraid he'll give me advice of his own. I can just imagine what it would be: *Go lie in the middle of Central Park in a glass coffin, looking so beautiful that a handsome prince can't help himself from kissing you.*

Not the most practical advice for a twenty-first-century teen girl living in New York City. Or, alternatively, he'll think I'm going wacko like Stepgrandma.

So I just give him a hug and say, "Oh, nothing." I put on my best Mom-imitation voice. "I just want to be my best self, the CharmingLifestyles.com way!"

Dad laughs.

"You really are your mother's daughter," he says.

But Mom got her handsome prince. And with a week and two days to go till the Fall Festive, I still have no date.

Chapter Eight

I MAKE A SPECIAL EFFORT WITH MY APPEAR- ance the next morning. With only one date candidate left, I have to step up my efforts. It's time to take this whole *Fairest in the Land* thing more seriously. When I'm dressed, I dig out the compact from the bottom of my backpack, survey myself in the Mirror, and pose the question:

Mirror Dear, Hello, good day,

Please tell me if I look okay.

The dance is soon, I need a date.

Help me before it is too late.

I know, I'm no Shakespeare. I stink at poetry. I just

hope my feeble rhymes are good enough for the Mirror.

Crickets . . .

My mouth is dry as I wait for the Mirror's verdict. I wonder if this is how Stepgrandma felt as she gazed at her reflection, waiting to hear if she really *was* the Fairest in the Land or if she came in second again.

That's when it hits me—the Mirror's opinion is starting to matter. The heavy gold compact is shaking in my hand as I wait to see if I pass muster.

You are the fairest, my Princess Rose.

Now the rest of the world shall know.

You shall not lack for dancing dates.

In fact, too many shall be your fate.

Are we talking boys? I snap the compact shut. I've got exactly one date candidate left, and he's not exactly promising, so I don't know what "too many shall be your fate" is supposed to mean.

Maybe the Mirror is like Dad and needs coffee before it makes sense in the morning.

Now I'm starting to think that an inanimate object needs coffee to wake up. . . .

Deciding I'm definitely going crazy like my stepgrandmother, I pick up my backpack, call good-bye to my parents, and head for school.

Damien Wolfe comes up to me in first period and thanks me for choosing him as my Kookie Kindness Day recipient yesterday.

"I mean, it's not like you know me that well, and . . . it was cool of you to do that," he says. "It worked some really good karma."

Yeah, for everyone else, I think.

But I plaster on a smile the Mirror would be proud of and say, "I'm happy to hear that."

Then he hands me a folded up piece of paper.

"I drew this for you."

I unfold it, and there's an original Damien Wolfe cartoon drawing of me with a cookie—which makes me look way better than I normally do, almost like a superhero version of me, that starts this big chain of smiley faces leading to other cookies and more smiley faces. A lump rises in my throat.

"Wow. That's . . . amazing," I manage to choke out around the lump.

"I just wanted to do something nice for you, because your giving me the cookies yesterday morning gave me the courage to finally ask Sophie to the Fall Festive," Damien confesses. "And she said yes!"

I pretend to be surprised. "I'm so happy for you!"

Funnily enough, I don't have to pretend the happy part as much as I thought I would.

On the way to my second period class, Quinn Fairchild pulls me to one side in the hall. I figure he wants to ask me something about Katie—like what kind of flowers she likes or something.

But he keeps his hand on my elbow as he leans up against the lockers, and he's standing a little too close for comfort; so close I can smell orange juice on his breath.

Quinn should brush his teeth after breakfast, or he's going to get cavities, I can't help thinking.

"Listen, Rosie, how about we go to the Fall Festive?" Quinn says.

I burst out laughing, and his hand tightens on my elbow. That's when I notice the shocked, angry look on his face and realize he was serious.

Pulling my elbow out of his grasp, I hiss, "Are you *crazy*? You already *have* a date, or have you forgotten that minor detail?"

Quinn tries to bluff his way out of it, like he's forgotten Katie and I are best friends.

"Who?"

"Katie Clark. You know, my best friend?"

"Oh. Well . . ." His brow wrinkles as he works his brain trying to come up with some believable excuse, like that's even possible. "Katie and I talked about going to the dance, but it wasn't, yanno, a hundred percent official."

"That's funny," I say. "Because I'm pretty sure *Katie* thinks it's a hundred percent official. In fact, I'm one hundred percent sure she thinks it is." I turn to go to class, but stop to look back at him over my shoulder and add, "There's no way I'd go out with my best friend's date. No way, nohow."

"I didn't know you were best friends," Quinn says.

"Then maybe you should show a little more interest in your date," I say before stomping off down the hall.

Worrying whether I should tell Katie what happened finally pushes anxiety about not having a date for the Fall Festive out of the top spot in the Things Rosie Is Freaking Out About list.

Katie's been super excited about going to the dance with Quinn. It's been the main topic of conversation ever since he asked her. What if I tell her, and it ruins everything? But what if I *don't* tell her, and then Quinn ends up hurting her because he's such a jerk?

I still haven't made up my mind when I get to the

cafeteria. When I join Katie and Nicole at the table, Katie is in midsentence.

"And I told Quinn that we should get matching roses—I'll wear mine in my hair and he can wear his in his buttonhole. What do you think, white roses or pink?"

"White," Nicole says. "I can't see Quinn agreeing to anything pink."

Katie sighs.

"I know. I wish he would, because pink is my favorite color."

I open my mouth to tell her that Quinn is a jerk who asked me to the dance after second period even though he was already going with her, but what comes out instead is, "You could always weave two miniature roses into your braid, one white and one pink."

"That's a fab idea, Rosie!" Katie exclaims. "I mean, I guess I should probably wait till I get the dress anyway. Oh, I've made a list of all the places I want to look on Saturday."

She whips out her phone and starts telling us all the stores we're going to hit on our Quest for the Dress.

And just like that, my moment for honesty is gone. I'll just have to hope that Quinn isn't as much of a jerk as I think he is, and that no one ever finds out that he asked me to the dance.

Mrs. Minnich gives back our *Romeo and Juliet* papers in Language Arts.

"Refreshing analysis, Rosie," she says, handing me back my response with a smile. I get an A minus and a smiley face.

I'm glad I didn't pretend to believe in all the *love at first sight* stuff to try to get a good grade and wrote what I really thought. So little about me feels honest right now.

"I'll be interested to hear your thoughts on 'Annabel Lee,'" she says.

We've started on our poetry unit, and the first poem we had to read was "Annabel Lee" by Edgar Allan Poe. The speaker is obsessed with Annabel, this girl who is from a kingdom by the sea. They meet as kids, and of course the guy is totally in *luuuurve* with Annabel and claims that she's just as obsessed with him. He says, *"And this maiden she lived with no other thought / Than to love and be loved by me."* I'm like, *seriously? All she ever thought about was loving him and being loved by him?* She never thought, *"I just read the best book EVER,"* or *"Wonder what my BFFs are* doing down in the village? #Letshangout" or "Does this ego-driven creep really believe the only thing I think about is him? #Stalker."

I was worried they were all going to be like this until Mrs. Minnich assigned us "Sonnet 43" by Elizabeth Barrett Browning. *"How do I love thee? Let me count the ways,"* she asks. Elizabeth B. B. loves purely and freely, *"as men strive for right."* But even though her poet husband, Robert, was the love of her life, I can't see Elizabeth B. B. having *no other thought than to be loved by him.* Because she wasn't just writing poems, she was campaigning for the abolition of slavery, even though her family's wealth had come from plantations in Jamaica that depended on it. All of that while she was sick with a lifelong chronic illness. Elizabeth Barrett Browning rocks.

I haven't run into Hunter Farthington all day, despite all my fashion-forward efforts, and it's now only eight days till the dance. I need to find him. So, as soon as school lets out, I race to the hallway where his locker is and casually walk by. He's hanging with his friends, and I just so happen to overhear Hunter saying he's going to Starcups to get an iced mocha before practice. I decide immediately that's where I'm going too.

As I follow Hunter out of the building at a discreet distance, I feel like an undercover spy trailing another agent.

Or, I realize to my horror, like a stalker. I don't want to be like "Annabel Lee" guy. So, once we're both out on the street, I scurry to catch up to him.

"Hey, Hunter, what's up? You heading to Starcups?"

"Yeah," he grunts, turning to acknowledge my presence and bashing me in the hip with his soccer bag.

"Ow!"

"Sorry."

"I'm heading there too."

"Cool," he says.

We walk side by side in awkward silence.

Okay, dating advice. Help!

I hear Uncle Bijou telling me: *Music is the soul of love. . . . Find out what rocks his soul and walk by singing that song.*

Rocks his soul . . . *Think, Rosie, think!*

Finally the brain wave strikes. Despite the fact that I know I am vocally challenged, I start singing "We Are the Champions."

I feel like an idiot when I start and even more like one when passersby give me the *just another weird New Yorker* glance. Hunter walks beside me, a hunky wall of silence.

I'm afraid to look at him. When we get to Starcups, he turns to me with a pained expression.

"Rosie, you're really cute," he says. "But singing . . . no. Definitely not your thing."

Ouch. Well, at least he said I was cute.

"Yeah, I know," I admit as we go inside.

Right away I notice Mystery Shakespeare Boy sitting in one of the comfy chairs by the window and reading a book. He looks up and sees me, and I wave hi and smile, but he doesn't seem to show any sign of recognition. His book is apparently more interesting than new, improved me. My fists clench. This isn't how it's supposed to work. What am I doing wrong?

"So, why do you sing if you know you're bad at it?" Hunter asks.

At that moment I realize that Hunter is the last person I want to be here with. I'm not even sure I want to go to the Fall Festive with him anymore, even though he's my final date candidate. Because even though I only sang because Uncle Bijou told me it might get me a date, and I knew deep down it was a really stupid idea, why shouldn't I sing even though I'm bad at it?

"I like singing," I tell him. "It makes me happy."

He shrugs.

"Just don't enter any singing competitions," he says. "You'd totally rock a beauty pageant, though. I'd, like, totally vote for you for Miss Teen America."

I can feel the compact stirring in the bottom of my backpack.

Princess Charming, doubting teen
Tell the Mirror what you've seen.
The handsome swain for you makes eyes.
The magic mirror never lies.

I'm in the middle of Starcups, so I can't get into an argument with the Mirror, but (a) the handsome swain still hasn't asked me to the Fall Festive, which was the whole point of this exercise and (b) what's the point of having a handsome swain if he tells me I shouldn't do things I like doing?

"Good to know," I tell Hunter.

Rosamunde Charming, Princess Teen
The fairest girl I've ever seen.
You could win a pageant grand
For you are the Fairest in the Land.

The Mirror is turning into one of those pushy Pageant Moms like in the reality TV shows.

The line is moving really slowly, because it's right after school and there's only one girl behind the counter taking orders. She looks miserable, wearing a black T-shirt, her dark, purple-streaked hair tied back, and a prominent nose ring sparkling on the side of her face. I'm standing with Hunter, but I don't really have anything to say to him, and the silence is making me uncomfortable. Maybe that's what makes me do it—because I have to find *something* to talk to him about.

"What about her?" I ask Hunter, nodding to the girl behind the counter. "Would you vote for her for Miss Teen America?"

Hunter laughs. Actually, it's more like an embarrassingly loud guffaw that I'm sure the girl behind the counter can hear—along with what he says next.

"What, that crow behind the counter? No way!"

"I know, right? A Vampira, Queen of the Night competition maybe," I add.

That makes Hunter laugh even louder. He even hits my upper arm to show his appreciation for my wit, the same way he would do to Quinn. Except I'm not Quinn, and I think I'm going to have a bruise.

I can almost hear the Mirror applauding in my backpack—or it would be applauding if it had hands, that is. The worse I behave, the more the thing seems to like me. Hunter's laughter and the Mirror's approval encourage me to keep talking. And the words that come out of my mouth surprise even me.

"Why would anyone get up in the morning and choose to dress that way? She might as well carry a sign saying, 'I'm a loser—don't talk to me.'"

"I know, right?" Hunter says. "It's just nasty."

I stroke down the skirt of my fashionable Phillipe-selected ensemble and toss my hair.

"I guess not everyone can be as stylin' as us, right?"

"Guess not," Hunter says.

It's finally our turn to order, so I don't have to force any more conversation. Hunter doesn't seem at all uncomfortable, but I can't make eye contact with Emo Girl because now that I'm up close, I'm worried that she heard us talking about her, and I feel bad.

She just takes my order and gives me my change. I say thank you and smile, even if I don't have the courage to meet her gaze.

"Gotta bolt," Hunter says, taking a sip of his iced mocha. "Can't be late for practice or Coach'll let me have it."

"Oh. Yeah. Good luck with the game tomorrow."

"You mean you're not coming to cheer me on?" Hunter asks. "It's home."

That's it! I realize. Katie told me I should pretend to be interested in his games. I just didn't realize pretending to be interested also entailed having to freeze my butt off on the sidelines and *watching*, but with the clock ticking down to the Fall Festive and me still being dateless, sacrifices must be made.

"I'll check my schedule," I say, giving him what I hope is my best Fairest in the Land smile.

"I'll look out for you," he says, flashing me a smile and winking as he turns to leave.

Victory!

I can't help feeling a sense of satisfaction that I've finally captured his interest. There's something to be said for the Fake Interest and Fairest Smile combo.

Princess Rose, I told you so,

These things the Mirror always knows.

This fine young man shall be your swain

By the eve of the next soccer game.

I wait for my skinny mocha, then glance over at Mystery Shakespeare Boy. He's still there by the window, reading. The chair opposite is empty. I casually stroll over and ask, "Is this seat taken?"

I smile and open my eyes wide, turning the power of

new, improved Mirror Girl up to full blast. Time to put this *Fairest in the Land* stuff to good use.

"No, go ahead," he says, barely looking up from his book.

Why is Mystery Shakespeare Boy immune to Mirror Girl's charms when she has such a strong effect on everyone else? What is the matter with him?

Taking a sip of my mocha, I feel around in the bottom of my backpack for the Mirror. I can't take it out, but feeling the jewels and the warm gold beneath my fingers gives me confidence. I *am* the Fairest in the Land now. The Mirror said so. It said I was the Fairest Girl it had ever seen.

I need to get his attention away from his book and on to me. I put the cup of coffee on the table between us and think of the dating advice I've received. Maybe singing? No, that was a total fail with Hunter. Buying him something to eat would be too obvious. Dancing in the middle of Starcups would be way too weird, not to mention embarrassing.

Across the café, a little kid knocks over his chocolate milk. The lid comes off, and it spills, and everyone at the table with him jumps up so it doesn't get on their clothes. It's certainly not the ideal way to get Mystery Shakespeare Boy's nose out of his book, but it could work.

So, I cross my legs and *accidentally on purpose* tap my coffee cup with my foot so that it spills all over the table.

"Omigosh, I'm *so* sorry!" I say, dabbing at the coffee daintily with my napkin. There's a lot more of it than I thought there would be. It's a pretty spectacular mess.

MSB jumps up as the mocha-y mess reaches his edge of the table, creating a chocolate splodge on the knee of his jeans.

He gives me a dirty look. This isn't going according to plan.

"I'll go get some more napkins," I say, rushing off to the counter and grabbing two handfuls of them. I go back to the table and throw napkins all over the coffee with one hand and start dabbing his knee with the other.

"I'm really sorry. I didn't mean to," I babble. "It was just one of those things. I can be a little klutzy at times, you know how it is. Sorry to interrupt your reading. Is it a good book?"

The whole time he's looking at me with this strange expression on his face. Then he grabs my wrist and moves my hand off his knee.

"Wait a minute. . . . Is that *you*?" he says, staring. "Ms. *Romeo isn't romantic; he's a player*?"

I'm standing there with a bunch of coffee-sodden paper towels in each hand, but I try to smile and look dignified, like the Fairest in the Land princess the Mirror keeps telling me I am.

"That would be me."

Mystery Shakespeare Boy's eyes widen.

"Wow. You sure got more than a haircut the other day," he says.

The male population of Manhattan World Themes Middle School has made it very clear that they like the new me better. My best friend's boyfriend asked me to the dance. But Mystery Shakespeare Boy's reaction is harder to read. I'm getting the sense that he's . . . not impressed.

"Well, I'm still the same old Rosie," I say.

He raises an eyebrow. He might have raised both, but there's that lock of hair that falls over his forehead in a most adorable way and hides the other one.

"What, you don't like my makeover?" I ask.

MSB shrugs.

"You're asking the wrong guy," he says, looking down at his low-key jeans and today's T-shirt, which reads *I* was addicted to the Hokey Pokey, but I turned myself around. "I'm not exactly Mr. Fashion."

"Even if you're not Mr. Fashion, you can have an opinion," I say.

He looks at me intently, and I feel like his eyes are seeing straight into my soul.

"You really want my opinion?"

"Yes, I do," I tell him, although I'm afraid now that I won't like the answer.

"In my opinion, the girl I thought I met the other day wouldn't have been so rude to the girl behind the counter. And that made her a whole lot prettier to me."

He picks up his bag and shoves his book into it.

"I gotta go."

And he walks out of Starcups, leaving me angry and confused.

Chapter Nine

AFTER TEXTING KATIE AND NICOLE TO SEE if they want to go to the soccer game tomorrow, I spend most of the evening in my room looking in the Mirror. I want to know what went wrong. I have to figure out why Mystery Shakespeare Boy was immune to my Fairest in the Land Charmingosity when most other boys seemed enchanted by it.

Magic Mirror, can you tell
Why the boy I like so well
Does not seem to bat an eye
When the fab new me walks by?

I look at my reflection from various angles as I wait for the Mirror to reply.

Fret not, Princess, you are Fair.

Over those small spots do not despair.

This serf is not the prince for you.

He is not fit to kiss your shoe.

Wow. That's seriously harsh. I might be mad at Mystery Shakespeare Boy, but calling him a serf is totally OTT. The Mirror is old. Maybe it doesn't understand that things are more PC these days. *All men are created free and equal* and all that.

Mirror, Mirror, family treasure,

I honor you beyond all measure.

But you can't just call a guy a serf.

These days we all have the same worth.

Oh no! Is that a zit on my nose now? I swear that just appeared out of nowhere. I wonder if the Mirror is giving me pimples as punishment.

Princess Rosie, you ignorant girl.

How little you know about the world.

You are the Princess, The Fairest, The One

And those who are not, they are just . . . scum.

I slam the compact shut.

All those stories I've heard about my stepgrand-mother's vanity and cruelty—that was the voice I heard just now from the Mirror.

It takes me a long time to fall asleep that night, and when I do, I dream of being buried under an avalanche of poisoned apples, but when I call for help, all I hear is the Mirror, laughing.

Mom and Dad are both in the kitchen when I go there for breakfast the next morning. They're still in their matching CharmingLifestyles.com silk bathrobes, each embroidered with a gold crown and a *C*. Dad's reading the *New York Times*, and Mom's engrossed in the Saturday *Wall Street Journal*. I'm already dressed in multiple layers, because I've got to go freeze in Central Park watching Hunter's soccer game.

"Make sure you take a hat and gloves," Mom says. "It's supposed to be very chilly today."

"Great," I groan. "Perfect weather for standing, watching a game for hours."

"I'm all for school spirit, but since when have you taken an interest in soccer?" Dad asks.

"Since my last candidate for a potential dance date

plays on the soccer team," I admit. "And since the dance is a week from today, and I still don't have a date."

"Ah . . . ," Dad says. "I see."

I can tell he's thinking, and that's always a worrying development when it comes to me and dating.

"I could come watch the game with you," Dad suggests. "Maybe I can encourage him to pop the question with my new CharmingMaster 15 Recurve Bow."

Mom and I look at each other, and then we both turn to Dad and say, "*No!*" in unison.

"Ivan, darling, you can't solve every problem with force," Mom says. "This calls for a more subtle approach."

"Except none of my subtle approaches seem to be doing any good," I sigh. "I tried following the uncles' advice and that didn't go so well."

My father snorts his coffee out through his nose.

"You asked *the Little Guys* for *dating advice*?"

"Ivan!" Mom gives him a hush-up look, but her rose-red lips are twisted in an attempt to hide a smile.

"Come on, Snow. Even *you* have to admit it's nuts," Dad sputters. "Asking seven workaholic guys for dating advice?"

"It's true, Rosie. You'd have been better off reading any one of my CharmingLifestyles.com pieces," Mom says. "I can't understand why you'd ask the uncles for advice rather than your own mother."

"I did ask you," I protest. "I got the makeover and I've been—"

I was about to say *I've been asking the Mirror for advice*, but then I remember Mom told me to keep it a secret. "Uh . . . I've been asking my friends for advice too. But it hasn't gotten me the desired result, and I'm running out of time."

"Don't worry," Mom says. "I'm sure *someone* will ask you. Anyway, these days aren't girls allowed to ask boys?"

Dad chokes on his orange juice. He's pretty old-fashioned about this stuff.

"I don't know," I say. "I mean, for Sadie Hawkins dances, yeah—but the *Fall Festive*?"

"Why not?" Mom says. "Don't you keep telling me how everything is different for you girls now? That you wouldn't be caught dead—or even *almost dead*—lying around in a crystal coffin waiting for some handsome prince?"

"But . . . but . . . ," I stutter, trying to come up with a retort.

"I think our dearest daughter has just been hoisted by her own petard," Dad chuckles.

I stare. "Hoisted by my *what*?"

"Your petard. It's a weapon we used once upon a time—you know, back in the old days when your mother and father were young," Dad explains with a twinkle in his eyes. "It was very useful for blowing up gates and walls when one was attacking a fortified castle."

"*You* attacked other people's castles?" I know Mom's all, like, Dad's her knight in shining armor, and he's still handsome—for a dad at least—but I've never seen him as a *blowing up walls* kind of guy.

"Only if they attacked mine first," Dad assures me. "But the phrase means that you were hurt by a weapon you meant to use to hurt others. Like your mom, for instance."

"Can I just eat breakfast?" I grumble. "I don't want to talk about this anymore."

I take a big bite of cereal as Mom and Dad exchange that *oh, teenagers* look with each other. It makes me want to use my spoon as a trebuchet (*See, Dad! I know some siege weaponry too!*) and catapult cereal at them until they stop.

But instead I shovel my breakfast down as fast as I can so that I can head to the park. As soon as I'm finished, I say, "Dad, no squirrel stalking anywhere near the soccer field, promise?"

"Understood, Dearest Daughter," Dad promises, but he

doesn't look happy about doing it. Nothing would make him happier than to appear on the edge of the soccer field with his CharmingMaster 15 Recurve Bow, looking ominous and flexing some princely muscle in Hunter's direction. Who knows, maybe he'd even set off a few of those petard thingies near the goalposts just to make his point.

Mom comes and kisses my forehead. Her lips are soft and warm.

"Make sure you wear gloves to keep your hands from getting chapped," she warns. "And a scarf to protect your neck."

"And a hat to keep the heat in and my hair from blowing around," I recite, escaping out the front door.

It's a relief to be outside in the cool air after the heat of my parent's expectations. As I walk the long blocks across to Central Park, I keep thinking about yesterday. About Mystery Shakespeare Boy and what he said. Every time I think about it, my stomach ties up in knots. I'm not the mean girl he thinks I am. The real me *is* the girl he met the first time.

Or is it?

Because those mean words did come out of my mouth, even if I don't feel good about having said them. I was just being Mirror Girl, doing what I thought I had to because I wanted Hunter to ask me to the dance.

I want MSB to like me.

That's the difference, I realize. The Mirror might consider Mystery Shakespeare Boy beneath me, but that's because it's from once upon a time.

Magic Mirror, need to upgrade.

Views go back to the Middle Ages.

It's a lame rhyme, but I don't have the courage to say it directly to the Mirror anyway.

I sigh and breathe in the crisp fall air, the smell of leaves starting to decay, and warm pretzels on the street carts. Time to pull myself together. Time to be Mirror Girl, smiling, happy, full of school spirit, whose only interest is that Manhattan World Themes Middle School wins the upcoming soccer match.

Go, Team!

I check my phone to see if Nicole or Katie has responded yet. There's a one word text from Nicole: *SERIOUSLY?!*

There's still no answer from Katie. Maybe she'll be at the game to cheer for Quinn, so maybe we can talk things through.

I text back to Nicole: *Seriously what?*

Have you forgotten something?

Forgotten what? I reply.

She doesn't answer. Whatever. I don't have time for her hissy fits right now. I've got to go fake some team spirit and hopefully snag myself a Fall Festive date.

When I get to the soccer field, Katie is nowhere to be seen. Genny Krulinski, on the other hand, is front and center. She's got a lawn chair set up right behind our team, and she's done her hair with ribbons in the school colors, complete with a matching scarf and gloves. I'm wearing a Manhattan World Themes sweatshirt, but my jacket covers it up. Sound the spirit *fashion faux pas* siren!

"Hi, Genny," I say, walking up to the sidelines.

"Oh . . . hi," she says. "Surprised to see you here."

"Hunter said I should come," I tell her.

"He did?" Genny clearly doesn't believe me. "When was that?"

"Yesterday afternoon. At Starcups."

"Oh."

"Do you come to a lot of games?" I ask her.

"Every home game," she says. "And some away games too."

"Wow. That's dedication," I say.

"I actually *like* soccer," she says.

And Hunter, I think.

But she's got a point. I'm the fraud on the sidelines, not Genny.

Then Hunter comes over.

"Hey, you showed up," he says.

"Yes," Genny and I chorus together.

He laughs.

"I knew *you'd* show up," he tells Genny. "You're always here. It's Rosie I wasn't sure about."

See, Princess, you must listen to me.

This young swain has eyes for thee.

He's handsome, strong, he'll do for now.

So smile and look pretty—you know how.

I don't want to hear the Mirror right now, especially because I see the hurt expression on Genny's face before she recovers and smiles brightly.

"I'm always here, because I'm your biggest fan," she says.

Hunter laughs.

"You girls can fight it out on the sidelines over who's my biggest fan," he says. "I've got a match to win."

With a cocky grin, he runs onto the field with the rest of the team to warm up. I'm surprised the size of his ego inflated head doesn't cause him to topple over.

"There's no competition," Genny says. "I'm his biggest fan."

I'm not about to argue with her. She's right. I'm becoming less of a Hunter fan the more I get to know him.

"I know."

She stares.

"You're agreeing with me?"

"Of course."

She looks like she's about to say something, but the referee's whistle blows, signaling it's time for kickoff. What comes out of her mouth is: "Let's go, Vikings!"

Yeah, we're the Manhattan World Themes Middle School *Vikings*—an odd mascot for a school whose mission statement is "to foster peace and understanding among all nations," right?

Whatever. I'm here to show my school spirit and get Hunter to ask me to the dance, not to ponder the ironic nature of our school mascot.

"Go, Vikings! Woo-hoo!" I shout, jumping up and down to denote extra enthusiasm. Also to increase the circulation in my toes, which are already starting to freeze, and the game has barely started.

And then I stand there, watching Hunter and the rest

of our team run up and down the field, back and forth and forth and back, kicking the soccer ball. There's a lot of whistle blowing and corner kicks, and something happens where the other team gets to kick straight at our goal while our guys stand in front of the goal with their hands over their private parts, which I find really amusing. But then Genny tells me it's called a penalty kick, and it's actually really bad for our side, especially when our goalie can't tip the ball away and it goes into the net and they score.

"I guess it's not that funny, then," I conclude.

"Uh . . . no. It's not funny at all," she says, shaking her head, like I'm a clueless soccer fan, which I am, basically.

I stick to following Genny's lead after that.

At halftime we're down 1–2. Our coach has the team huddle around him, and it sounds like he's giving them a cross between a pep talk and a reading of the riot act.

My toes are starting to freeze. I'm not sure if I can handle another half. At least the players are running around, so they get to stay warm.

Genny came prepared. She's obviously done this before. Not only does she have the chair, she's got a stadium blanket covering her legs, snacks, and a thermos of hot chocolate. My stomach is rumbling, and I'd give anything for a hot drink.

I try doing jumping jacks and running in place. At least I can feel my toes again.

My fingertips are numb, but I take out my cell and check to see if my friends have texted me. There's still no word from Katie, and nothing more from Nicole. Something is definitely up with them. I just wish I knew what it was.

The second half goes more quickly. Well, not really, but maybe it seems that way, because we start scoring more goals, and I'm finally starting to understand what's going on. It's easier to cheer when you know what to cheer for. If I didn't feel like parts of my body might fall off from the cold, I might actually enjoy myself. *Note to self: Cute little flats are not optimal soccer watching wear. Warm boots and thick socks are more appropriate.*

Hunter scores a goal in the last two minutes, making the score 4–2 in our favor. He's carried off the field in triumph. I go over to congratulate him while Genny's packing up all her soccer watching gear.

"Thanks for coming," he says. "Looks like you brought good luck."

I laugh, because the idea of me, who barely knows anything about the game, bringing any kind of good fortune, is pretty hilarious.

"I doubt that, but thanks."

"Listen, how about going to the Fall Festive?" Hunter asks, like it's no biggie.

Goal! Score! Go, Rosie!

"Sure, okay," I reply, trying to sound equally as laid back.

"Cool," he says. "Well, I gotta go."

He gestures toward his teammates.

"We always go for pizza after the game."

"Yeah, sure. See you at school."

Genny is coming toward us, and I take off down the path toward home before she arrives.

I kick a stone along the path as I walk away from the playing fields, letting my foot vent my frustration. I finally have a date for the Fall Festive! I've achieved what I set out to do.

So, why don't I feel happier about it?

I actually feel *guilty* about Hunter asking me instead of Genny. She really likes him. She's the one who goes to every soccer game to watch him play. She knows what's going on, while I'm laughing when our side has a penalty kick against us.

But Hunter asked *me. It's what I wanted,* I remind myself.

I should text Nicole and Katie to tell them the good news, but since Nicole has been sending me cryptic messages and Katie is giving me the cold shoulder, I don't know who to tell.

Besides, my toes feel like they're about to break off with each step, and my fingertips are numb inside my gloves. I'm not sure I could text anyone, even if I wanted to.

None of this has turned out the way I expected.

"Is that little Rosie Charming I spy on the path before me?"

The familiar deep voice comes from a huge clump of bushes beside the path.

"Harold? Is that you?" I call out. "Where are you hiding?"

Leaves rustle and part. Harold the Huntsman emerges from the bushes, dressed in his usual forest-green wool, with bits of shrubbery sticking to his sleeves and twigs caught in his long, graying hair and beard.

"Rosie," he says, his weathered face split with a wide smile, which reaches his focused green eyes. Harold's eyesight is famous; he can spot prey at an incredible distance—or at least he could in his youth, according to my parents and the uncles. "What brings you to this part of Central Park?"

"A soccer game," I say. "What about you?"

"Rat stalking," Harold sighs. "It's a comedown after being a royal huntsman chasing deer and wild boar, but it works as a retirement job."

He sits on the nearest bench and pats the seat next to him, gesturing for me to sit down.

I slump onto the bench. He takes one of my small, chilled hands into his big ones. I can feel the warmth even through his worn leather gloves embossed with the same royal crest that's on my compact.

"Have you got your horn on you?" Harold asks.

"Yes," I say, pulling the small gold horn he gave me out of my bag. I never go anywhere without it. Harold gave it to me when I was six. He said it's for emergencies—to call him with when I'm in danger. Like a super old-fashioned cell phone.

Harold smiles.

"Good. Don't ever leave home without it. You never know when evil might strike."

"I'll say," I agree as I put the horn back in my bag.

"Especially when you live in New York City."

"You look more like your mother every day," Harold says, shaking his head wonderingly. "It's uncanny. Brings back memories . . . of that day in the forest. . . ."

He shudders. Clearly, these aren't good memories. Then I realize what he's talking about.

"You mean the day you were supposed to kill Mom?"

"Yes, Rosie. The day that haunts my dreams. I still see my arm raised, holding the knife, and her face looking up at me—so innocent, so confused, so . . . terrified."

He's so upset that I don't have the heart to tell him that Mom still dreams about it too. I've been woken up by her screams: *No! Please don't kill me! Please!*

I decide to ask him a question that's been bothering me ever since I heard the story—and especially since I read The Tale as it's told in books.

"Did you really just let her go because of her looks?"

Harold looks shocked, and I wonder if I've upset him. But then he laughs.

"Well, her face certainly *was* the fairest I'd ever seen," he admits. "But that wasn't the only reason I let her go."

"So, why did you?" I ask.

"Well, because unlike her stepmother, Snow White was kind. She spoke to everyone at the Castle with respect, whether they be a highborn lord of the court or a lowborn servant scrubbing the floor," Harold tells me. "She thanked people for their service, instead of taking it as her due."

I think about how I treated the girl behind the counter in Starcups. If Stepgrandmom sent Harold to kill *me*, would I have been nice enough to be spared?

"Your mother could have been like the Queen, her stepmother—beautiful on the outside but rotten to the core. But she wasn't," Harold continues. "She still isn't. She's good inside and out. I didn't spare her because of her looks. It was because of her deeds."

I don't know who or what to believe anymore. What I *do* know is that the storybooks lied.

Chapter Ten

KATIE AND NICOLE DON'T RESPOND TO me on Sunday, either. I text asking what is wrong, but neither of them reply. I call, but they both let it go straight to voice mail. I get the impression I've done something really, really bad, but I have no idea what it is.

Mom's excited to hear I have a date though. Dad, on the other hand, wants to meet him and interrogate him before I'm allowed to go to the dance. Mom tells Dad to lighten up. She wants to take me to Très Cher to go dress shopping right away, but I put her off, even though the dance is less than a week away. I'm just not in the mood for more shopping and beautification.

"At least find out what color flower he needs for his boutonniere," Mom says. "We need to order it."

"Can't we just get a flower from the corner store and stick a pin in it?" I ask.

Mom gives Dad an *Ivan, you deal with this* look.

"No, dear, you can't. It would get flower stem residue all over his jacket," Dad says.

Silly me. How could I have ignored the dangers of flower stem residue?

"Men have sartorial considerations too, you know," Dad reminds me. "You ladies aren't the only ones who have to cut a fine figure."

"Sar-what?"

"We care about clothes and looking good too," Dad explains.

"Yeah, but it's easier for you," I complain. "You don't have to wear makeup or heels, and no one gives you confusing advice like: *Be charming and funny—but not too flirtatious or you might get a reputation you don't want.*"

My parents stare at me.

"Who gave you *that* advice?" Mom asks.

"Um . . . I googled it," I mumble.

There's silence. Mom's face looks like she swallowed

a lemon. Dad's is slowly turning a darker shade than Mom's Red as Blood nails.

"What?" I ask.

Dad explodes into guffaws, and Mom into helpless giggles.

My parents are laughing at me. So hard, in fact, that Mom can barely stand up, and she has to cling to Dad's arm for support.

"She . . . *googled* . . . *it!*" Mom gasps, wiping tears from her eyes.

"*I don't need Dear Old Dad! I've got The Google!*" Dad says in a high voice that is supposedly me.

I've had enough.

"It's GOOGLE, not *THE* Google," I shout, stomping out of the kitchen to my room. I make sure to slam the door to my room extra hard so they hear it over their Laugh at RosieFest.

If I make a pros and cons list of my life at the moment, it would look something like this:

Pros

An old family heirloom tells me I'm the Fairest in the Land.

My Kookie Kindness Day lie made school a nicer place for

a day and gave Damien Wolfe the courage to ask someone to the dance.

I have a date for the Fall Festive.

Cons

I don't like my date for the Fall Festive all that much.

My parents are laughing at me because I googled dating advice.

I'm being frozen out by my best friends, and I don't know why.

Mystery Shakespeare Boy thinks I'm a jerk.

I'm starting to wonder if maybe I am one.

I take out the Mirror and gaze at my reflection. What is the matter with me? Even if the Mirror is wrong, and I'm not the Fairest in the Land (there are 320 million people in the United States, so you have to admit that's a pretty tall order), I'm not bad-looking.

So why has everything in my life started going so spectacularly wrong?

Mirror, what use is being fair

If my besties do not care?

And people think that I'm not nice.

Is beauty just too great a price?

The Mirror takes its time giving me an answer, and I get even more depressed, wondering if it has ditched me too. I'm considering throwing the stupid thing across the room when finally it speaks:

Rosie Charming, Princess, Teen,
The Fairest Girl I've ever seen,
Ignore the haters, they just envy
'Cause the boys, they being friendly.

Ugh. The Mirror is starting to sound like Dad when he's trying to be cool and failing miserably.

But I wonder if it's right, and Katie and Nicole are jealous about the attention I've been getting since my appointment with Phillipe.

I guess I'll find out tomorrow.

As I look out the bus window two blocks before the school stop, I see Katie walking alone, and I ring the buzzer so I can get off and walk with her. She's half a block ahead of me by the time I push my way out of the rush hour crowd, so I have to run to catch up.

"Hey, Katie!" I gasp.

I might be the Fairest in the Land, but I need to get into better shape if I'm going to be chasing after friends while carrying a full book bag and wearing ballet flats. These shoes aren't made for running.

"Rosie." Katie says my name with all the warmth of a polar vortex. "Hey." She picks up her pace.

"Katie, what's wrong?" I ask, grasping her arm so she has to stop.

"Seriously?" she asks, wrenching her arm away. "Like you don't *know*?"

"Seriously. If I *knew*, I wouldn't have to ask." I look into her eyes, hoping that she'll see the sincerity in mine. "*Please*. Why are you so mad at me?"

My friend stares at me as if still unable to believe I don't know.

"Well, first of all, you blew us off on Saturday."

Saturday? What is she talking about? I was at Hunter's soccer match, freezing my butt off and scoring a date to the dance.

Katie starts walking away.

"You *still* don't remember that we were supposed to go dress shopping, do you?"

Her words hit me like a slap across the face—one that I deserve. I can't believe I forgot. I am the worst friend *ever*.

"Katie, I'm sorry. I'm a total idiot," I call out. "Please, wait up."

She slows but doesn't stop, and I hurry after her, trying to explain.

"I've been so obsessed with trying to get a date for the Fall Festive that I spaced," I grovel. "I feel awful. I'm so, *sooooo* sorry."

Katie stops finally, and I experience a second of hope. It's short-lived.

"That's not the only thing. Genny Krulinski heard Quinn asking you to the Fall Festive," she bites out through clenched teeth. "How could you flirt with him when you knew we were going together?"

Omigosh. The Mirror is right. She is *jealous*, I think. And the irony is that she has absolutely no reason to be. I wouldn't go out with Quinn Fairchild if you paid me— even if Katie weren't seeing him.

"Katie, I never flirted with Quinn. Of course I wouldn't do that! You're my best friend!"

"But you're not denying that he asked you?" Her voice is angry, but I can see the understandable hurt in her eyes.

"Well . . . no, but—"

"Why didn't you tell me?"

Good question.

I *should* have told her as soon as it happened. I realize that now, of course. But at the time . . .

"You were so excited about going with him. You were talking about the roses . . . what color and . . . I just . . . didn't want to ruin things."

It sounds like a lame excuse, even to me. And *I* know it's the truth.

Katie's skeptical look tells me she doesn't believe me.

"So, you decided to keep something this important a secret from your best friend?" she says. "Right. And I suppose you were totally surprised that he asked you too."

"*I was!*" I protest. "It came totally out of the blue. And the first thing I said to him was that I thought he was already going with you!"

"But you didn't say no!"

"*Yes*, I did!"

"That's not what I heard," Katie says.

"But it's the *truth*," I say, desperate for her to believe me, because it is the truth.

"I don't think you even know what that word means," Katie snorts. She turns her back on me and walks away as fast as she can, crossing the street to school.

Tears blur my vision as I watch my best friend disappear into the crowd of students. Ducking into the doorway of a store that still hasn't opened for the day, I pull a tissue out of my backpack and pull out the Mirror. Looking at my reflection, I blot my eyes so it doesn't look like I've been crying.

Mirror, Mirror, wise old glass,
Why have these bad things come to pass?
My best friend thinks that I'm a liar.
This Fairest business has misfired.

The Mirror suddenly feels warm in my fingers.

Silly Princess, do not weep,
Friends like this you should not keep.
Although things might feel out of hand
It's worth it to be Fairest in the Land.

Snapping the compact shut, I shove the Mirror to the bottom of my backpack.

For the first time I wonder if the Mirror is wrong.

It sure doesn't feel worth it being Fairest in the Land right about now.

I catch Nicole by her locker before school starts, but only because she didn't see me first. She almost slams the locker door on my fingers when she realizes it's me.

"Are you mad at me because Quinn asked me to the Fall Festive too?" I ask.

"What do you think?" she says. "*And* you blew us off

on Saturday. You're not exactly killing it in the friendship department."

"I know. I feel awful. But I said *no* to Quinn," I tell her. "And I *wasn't* flirting with him. Katie's my friend."

"A friend would tell her best friend that the guy she thinks she's going out with is hitting on someone else. Especially when it's *that friend*," Nicole points out.

"Okay, I messed up big time by not saying anything when it happened," I admit. "But Katie was so excited about going with him. I didn't want to rain on her parade."

"You'd rather let her go with some jerk who asks out her best friend behind her back?"

"No, but—"

"And why did he ask you anyway?" Nicole asks. "He already had a date. Katie. So he's going to just out of the blue ask you?"

"I don't know!" I exclaim. "I'm as surprised and confused about it as you are."

"I don't think you are," Nicole says.

"What do you mean by that?"

Nicole half turns to leave, like she can't wait to get away from me.

"I mean . . . you've been *different* lately, Rosie," she says. "And *not* in a good way."

And she takes off down the hall without giving me a chance to defend myself.

Not that I would have known what to say in my own defense.

Being the Fairest in the Land sure isn't all it's cracked up to be.

I can't sit with Katie and Nicole at lunch, since they aren't talking to me. I could do with some Kookie Kindness right about now, but no one's giving *me* any. So I buy myself a cookie and take it to the girls' bathroom to eat.

I can just imagine the CharmingLifestyles.com sidebar listicle about this:

3 Reasons Why Bathroom Eating Is a Big No-No!

1) Germs, Germs, Germs!!

2) Bathrooms are for relieving yourself, not for nourishment. Multitasking has its place, and it's not in the restroom!

3) Eating is a social activity. What you do in the bathroom is private. TMI isn't Charming, ladies!

But right now my fear of germs is overcome by the

need to be alone so I can think, and a bathroom stall is the only place where solitude is guaranteed.

I put a book on my lap and spread a paper napkin over it like a tablecloth before unwrapping my cookie. I am my mother's daughter after all, and I have to give my meal some semblance of Charmingness, despite eating in a bathroom.

But even the cookie doesn't make me feel better. Maybe it's missing the kindness part. Or maybe my problems go beyond anything a cookie can solve.

After I finish eating, I reach into my backpack and pull out the compact. It's so ornate and bejeweled it seems even more wrong to open the Mirror in here than it did to eat. But I need answers.

The Rosie reflected in the Mirror looks sad. Her eyes don't have their usual light, and that's not just because we're in a bathroom stall under unflattering fluorescents.

Mirror in my family for so long,
What if maybe you are wrong?
And this is all a big mistake
That is just causing me heartache?

My voice breaks on the last word, and a tear rolls down my cheek. The compact starts vibrating in my hand, so violently that I'm afraid I'm going to drop it and then I'll have to worry about seven years of bad luck as well as all the disgusting germs on the bathroom floor.

How dare you doubt me, Princess Rose!

The future is what the Mirror knows.

Go fix your face, you look a fright

And remember—THE MIRROR IS ALWAYS RIGHT!

The Mirror stills when it finishes speaking.

Now it's my fingers that are trembling as I close the compact and put it in my bag.

I think the Mirror is lying. And I'm going to find out why.

I can barely think about anything else for the rest of the school day. As soon as the final bell rings, I head for Central Park to seek out Harold the Huntsman. He still hasn't given in to having a cell phone, but I have the emergency horn. I don't know if this officially qualifies as a hornworthy emergency, but it sure feels like one. So I stand in the middle of the Great Lawn and sound the thing like Harold taught me all those years ago, feeling like a total dork when people stare. I wonder if I should just put down a hat and pretend I'm a busker. Then nobody would look twice, because this is New York City and anything goes.

Less than five minutes after the final blast, Harold comes running down the path toward me, his eyes searching for the imminent threat.

"Why are you standing in such an unprotected spot if you're in danger?" he scolds. "You should be looking for cover. Come!"

He shields me under his arm and hastens down the path toward the shelter of the trees, taking such big strides I have to run to keep up.

"Wait . . . Harold. It's not that kind of danger," I pant between breaths. "Let's just . . . sit here a minute." I point to the nearest park bench.

Harold scopes out the area around the bench and looks up and down the path for anything or anyone he deems a threat to my safety. When he's convinced that there's nothing more dangerous than a squirrel nearby, he nods and we sit.

I pull the jeweled compact out of my backpack and show it to him.

"Have you ever seen this before?"

His eyes widen at the sight of all the jewels, but he shakes his head.

"I recognize the crest, of course—it's the coat of arms of your mother's royal line," Harold says. Rolling up his coat, he points to his leather glove, and the same coat of arms is embossed there. "But I have never laid eyes on that. Where did you get it?"

"My mother gave it to me," I tell him. "It's got this Mirror inside," I say opening it up. "And it's really weird because it talks to me."

Harold gasps. Actually, it's more of a choke. It scares me because it sounds like he's about to keel over.

"Rosamunde! You must get rid of it right away."

I stare at him, shocked by his vehemence. His normally ruddy face is pale. He's starting to freak me out.

"Why? What is it?"

He reaches out one of his large hands, pointing to the Mirror. The steadiest hand in the Wood Beyond the Seven Mountains is trembling like a leaf in an autumn breeze. "Close it."

I do as he asks.

"Rosie, please. Get rid of that. Destroy it. It will bring you no happiness."

"But I can't. My mother gave it to me."

His eyes widen, and his skin loses another shade of color. "*Snow White* gave this to you?"

I nod slowly, in contrast to the rapid beating of my heart.

"I don't understand," Harold says, rising to his feet

and pacing away from me. I hear him muttering: "Why would she . . . What strange evil . . . I thought—"

He spins and turns back to me.

"Rosie, I do not understand your mother's purpose. But if you never believe me on anything, trust me on this: Get rid of that mirror." He shudders. "I cannot be in its presence any longer. I must go. Mark my words, Rosie. That Mirror is evil."

The gold compact is heavy in my hand, but my heart feels even heavier as I watch Harold walk away from me briskly, as if I'm contagious with a deadly plague. I tell myself it's the Mirror he doesn't like, not me, but after what happened in school today, I'm starting to wonder.

I put the compact in my pocket, where it rests like a heavy weight, and walk across the park to West Seventy-Seventh, hoping that the uncles are home. There's no answer when I ring the bell, and I'm starting back up the steps to walk to catch the crosstown bus back home when Uncle Shrimpy shouts "Rosie! What a fantastic surprise!" from street level.

"I hope you still think so after I tell you what I came here for," I say.

Uncle Shrimpy smiles, taking out his keys and opening the front door. "I always love spending time with you, Rosie."

He's so genuinely happy to see me that I burst out crying.

Shrimpy puts his arm around my waist (which is a reach for him), brings me inside, and guides me to the sofa to sit.

"Hey, honey . . . What's all this about?" he says, climbing up on the seat next to me so he can reach my shoulder to pat it comfortingly. "Still having boy problems?"

"I'm h-having *e-everything* p-problems," I wail.

Shrimpy passes his handkerchief, which he assures me is clean. Given the stories Mom's told me about the uncles' personal hygiene when she met them, I'm not sure I believe him, but I take it anyway, because tears are dripping off my nose and chin.

"Everything problems are overwhelming," Shrimpy says, his voice low and gentle. "I can understand why you're crying."

He taps my knee with his finger.

"I'm not sure I can help with Everything problems," he sighs. "But how about you start by telling me about one problem? Sometimes I can figure out how to deal with things if I take it one step at a time."

A week ago I would have said my biggest problem was not having a date for the Fall Festive. But now that doesn't even seem like such a big deal when I think about the fact that Katie thinks I would flirt with her boyfriend and Nicole says I'm different in a bad way. Or that I think—and Harold's behavior seems to have confirmed—that there's something sinister about the Mirror my mother gave me.

The jeweled compact is still weighing down my pocket. I pull it out and hand it to Uncle Shrimpy.

"I don't know what to do about this," I tell him. "Mom gave it to me, but Harold the Huntsman says I should get rid of it."

Shrimpy's eyes light up at the sight of the gemstones inlaid in the gold. From under his shirt he draws out a jeweler's loupe that he wears on a chain around his neck and starts examining the quality of the diamonds.

"Near colorless and almost flawless—I'd bet you any money that these diamonds came from the Seven Mountains Mine!" he exclaims. "I haven't seen stones of this quality since we came to New York City."

He looks at the rubies, sapphires, and emeralds too.

"You say Snow White gave this to you?" he asks. "That makes sense. We gave her and Prince Charming a chest of precious gems from the mines as a wedding present. Be careful walking around the city with this. The gems alone are worth a fortune."

As if I didn't have enough to worry about, now I can add Being Mugged to the list.

"Open it," I say.

He opens the compact and sees the Mirror. His reaction is the same as Harold's. He drops the compact into my lap like it singed his fingers.

"Where did you get that?" he asks in a tremulous voice.

"I *told* you. Mom gave it to me."

"Why?" he asks.

"I don't know," I say. "She said . . . she said she'd been waiting for the right time and now seemed good. Or something like that."

"Never would be the right time," Shrimpy says. "It is a source of great unhappiness."

He's right. I mean, look what's happened since it's been in my possession. I might be the Fairest in the Land, but my best friends aren't speaking to me.

Still, when I hold it, the weight in my hand is strangely comforting, and I find myself reluctant to part with it.

"But you just said the jewels alone are worth a fortune," I argue.

The compact vibrates in my hand like a purring cat, telling me we belong together.

"What use is fairness and fortune if you are all alone?" Shrimpy says. "Look what happened to your stepgrandmother, the Queen."

How could I forget?

You've probably seen the movie version of The Tale, which is "based on a true story," but certain pertinent facts were changed so they could have a Hollywood ending, or in this case so they could get a G rating from the Motion Picture Association of America.

See, the dwarves didn't really chase Stepgrandma over a cliff. Dad's parents invited her to Mom and Dad's wedding, but Stepgrandma didn't realize the bride was Mom. Before she went, she asked the Mirror the same old question: *Mirror, Mirror, on the wall, who in this realm is the fairest of all?*

She wasn't that worried about the answer, because she thought she'd killed Mom with the poisoned apple, and from what she'd heard from passing travelers, Mom was still firmly ensconced in the glass coffin in the middle of the woods, surrounded by sad little men.

But then Dad came along and did his creepy kissy

thing and lo and behold! True love! So my parents were having this big ole white wedding and before Stepgrandma left, she was primping before the Mirror and expecting the usual answer but instead she got:

You, my queen, may have a beauty quite rare,

But Snow White is a thousand times more fair.

So Stepgrandma had a conniption and almost didn't go to the wedding, but curiosity doesn't just kill cats, apparently. She went, and Dad's parents had these special iron slippers waiting for her, because Mom and Dad had told them how she'd tried to kill Mom. As soon as she arrived, all dressed in her best party outfit and thinking she was at least the second Fairest in the Land if not the Fairest, they forced her to put on these iron shoes, and they were so hot (because they'd been heated over a fire) that Stepgrandma started dancing, because her feet hurt so much. And she danced and she danced while everyone else stood in a circle and clapped and cheered (because they didn't realize she was wearing the iron slippers; they just thought she was this attractive woman with some really fly moves), and then all of a sudden she collapsed and died. Heart attack.

Pretty harsh, right? I was seriously freaked out the first

time I heard The Tale, but Mom said at least the shoes were made by Fanolo Branik, a distant ancestor of the famous shoe designer.

"But Dad's parents *tortured* Stepgrandma!" I exclaimed. "Even if it was with red-hot designer shoes!"

"Can I remind you that Stepgrandma tried to *kill me*? Not just once but *three times*? What did you want us to do?" Mom asked.

"I don't know—couldn't you just have put her in the dungeon for thirty to life?" I argued.

Mom and Dad said I just didn't understand. Things were different once upon a time.

"I should probably head home," I say, getting up to leave instead of giving Shrimpy an answer. Because I don't have an answer for him. Even if he's right, I'm not sure I can give up the Mirror.

"Please, Rosie. Listen to your uncle Shrimpy, not the Mirror."

I know Uncle Shrimpy is much smarter than everyone gives him credit for, but the Mirror is vibrating in my pocket, as if to say *Keep me. Keep me.*

So I just hug Shrimpy and say, "Thanks for listening."

Then I head out to catch the crosstown bus, with the Mirror still safely in my pocket.

Chapter Eleven

AT DINNER LAST NIGHT I THOUGHT ABOUT asking Mom what Harold the Huntsman and Uncle Shrimpy couldn't understand—why she would give me the compact with the Mirror. From the way they've been freaking out, I'm getting a sneaking suspicion that it might be part of *the* Mirror—the one that belonged to Stepgrandma. There's that constant urging that I should strive to be the Fairest in the Land, not to mention the Mirror's insistence that I talk to it in rhyme. The clues are adding up.

But Mom and Dad were all excited about a big new contract they'd signed with CynCorp for a new line of CharmingLifestyles.com *mirror*s, of all things. Tag-line: *See Your Best Self with the Fairest range of mirrors from CharmingLifestyles.com.*

"We just paid for your college tuition with today's deal," Mom says.

Dad was really proud of Mom, because she'd negotiated the entire deal—and haggled with the CynCorp guys to get higher percentages for the use of the Charming name.

"Your mom isn't just a pretty face, Rosamunde," he said, giving Mom a mushy look as he held hands with her across the table. "She's a sharp businesswoman, too!"

"I guess she's learned from the mistakes she made in those business transactions with Stepgrandma," I said.

"Rosie! That was uncalled for," Dad snapped.

My mother just looked at me, her blue eyes wide, confused, and . . . hurt.

"Sorry," I mumbled.

But I wasn't, really. I wanted to hurt her. Because she gave me that stupid jeweled compact, and that's why I'm in this mess.

I *knew* asking my mother for dating advice was a bad idea.

After tossing and turning most of the night, I'm still

angry. So mad that I wear my Converse with one of Phillipe's outfits, as an act of protest, instead of the ballet flats that are supposed to go with it. Heads are probably exploding on Fifty-Ninth Street at this very moment because of my fashion sacrilege. But it makes me feel better to wear something from my life before the Mirror.

A ray of morning sunlight filters through my bedroom window and catches the gems on the compact, which is lying on my bedside table, refracting a rainbow of colors around the room. It's almost . . . magical. Telling myself that this has to be a sign of some kind, I pick up the compact and open it. Mirror Girl stares back it me. I should be totally used to her, but sometimes, even now, I look in the Mirror and have a hard time believing that she's me.

Mirror, Mirror, what should I do?
People say to get rid of you.
Since you have come into my life
It has been filled with lots of strife.

Okay, so asking the Mirror for advice about getting rid of itself probably isn't the brightest idea I've ever had, but the Mirror tells me I'm the Fairest in the Land, not the Smartest.

Spoiled Princess! How can you so inquire?

Claiming I, the Mirror, have made your life dire?
Because of me, you now have a date,
So cease this complaining, you whiny ingrate!

Usually the Mirror responds in a quatrain—or is it a quadruplet? Whatever, four lines of poetry. But now it's so mad at me it's doubling down. This time I get double the "fun."

And while we're at it, oh please, girl, those shoes!
Just looking at them gives this Mirror the Blues.
Has my confidence in you, Rosie, been completely displaced?
Are you letting your Fairest potential go to waste?

I shut the compact, just in case the Mirror plans to keep nagging me. Like I don't already feel bad enough about myself. Besides, it's time to leave for school.

From the window of the bus I can see Hunter standing with his soccer buddies in their usual spot. Shouldn't my pulse start to beat a little faster at the sight of him? Katie was so excited about going to the dance with Quinn. He might be a total jerk, but he's a jerk that she really likes. Shouldn't I feel something other than wanting to run in the opposite direction as fast as my beat-up sneakers will take me?

But there's a dance on Saturday, and he's my date, for better or for worse, and Mom says I have to ask him what color flower he wants for his lapel. Personally, I think the boutonniere thing is overkill, but Mom insists it isn't. Katie was stressing out about flower colors back when we were still talking, so I'm going with the program.

After getting off the bus, I try taking a deep calming breath before I approach Hunter, but end up inhaling bus fumes and coughing instead of calming. I cough so much, I have to dig a tissue out of my backpack to wipe tears out of my eyes, and as I do, I see Genny Krulinski sidle up to Hunter, smiling. He grins back at her, and by the time I've put the tissue in the garbage, they are chatting away.

Hunter seems to have a whole lot more to say to her than he does to me, I think.

Maybe it's because she's actually interested in the things that he says to her. Maybe it's because she really likes him, and I . . . don't.

Hunter and I don't have anything in common—the only things we've ever talked about are him and that poor girl at Starcups—and I feel bad about doing that.

I don't actually want to go to the dance with him, even if it means I don't go at all, I realize all of a sudden. I'd rather just stay home and watch a movie. Or read a book.

This decision is going to make the Mirror's head explode—or it would, if the Mirror actually had a head. But I feel like I've just been told I don't have to take a test I didn't study for, the relief is so great. Except now I have to figure out how to break the news to Hunter.

I stress about it all day in school, looking for the right opportunity. His soccer buddies always surround him, or Genny is right there. There's no easy way to do this, I realize by the end of the day.

So, I take a deep breath and go up to him as he's standing by his locker with two guys from the team.

"Hunter, can I talk to you for a minute?"

"Sure, go ahead," he says.

"I mean, alone."

"Oooooh, alone!" his teammate teases. "How romantic!"

Hardly, I think.

Hunter punches him on the arm and tells him to get lost—he'll meet them out front in five minutes.

Then he leans up against the locker and says, "So, what's up?"

I've been waiting to do this all day. But now that I'm looking Hunter in the face, it's not so easy to do.

"Hunter, I'm sorry."

"About what?"

"I can't go to the dance with you."

"Oh, okay."

Okay?

It's not like I wanted him to be upset, but I was expecting a little more than "Oh, okay."

"Anyway, I was thinking, maybe you should ask Genny Krulinski."

Hunter nods.

"Good idea. Thanks."

"No problem."

"I gotta split," he says. "Practice."

"Sure. Have fun."

He laughs.

"'Fun' isn't what I'd call it, but yeah."

Genny would know the right thing to say to him about practice instead of "Have fun." I hope he does ask her. And I'm relieved that I don't have to go to the dance and spend hours trying to figure out what to say to him.

I decide to celebrate my decision—and console myself

for once again being dateless, even if it is by choice—by treating myself to a large mocha at Starcups. On the way there, I pass the drugstore and catch sight of my reflection in the window. I stop to look, because even after a week, I still don't think of the girl I see there as me. Maybe it's time to change that.

Mom's not going to like my decision, but I go into the store and head to the hair color aisle. I pick up a box of temporary Purple Haze hair rinse, but decide that might be pushing it. Instead, I pick a color like my hair used to be, before Phillipe and Giacomo did their thing with it. By dinnertime tonight, I hope to feel like my old self.

When I get to Starcups, I hit the ladies' room before ordering, and as I wash my hands afterward, I smile at my reflection in the mirror over the sink. At least I know this mirror isn't going to talk back to me. I'm tired of being berated by a piece of reflective glass.

Maybe Shrimpy and Harold are right. Maybe I *should* get rid of the Mirror.

I take the compact out of my backpack. It's so beautiful, with its burnished gold casing and gemstones, which even under the dim bathroom lighting glow with an inner fire. I trace the engraving of Mom's family coat of arms with my finger and then grab a few paper towels from the dispenser. After wrapping the compact carefully, I take deep breath and throw it in the trash.

I pick up my backpack and exit the restroom. But before the lady who is waiting with her cross-legged toddler can go in, I turn around and run back in, lock the door, and dig the compact out of the garbage can. Unwrapping it, I wipe it gently with a damp towel and then wash my hands before stowing it safely in the bottom of my backpack.

It is a family heirloom, after all, given to me by my mother. As much as I hate the thing, I can't just throw it in the garbage in a public restroom. It's . . . undignified. Especially for something that old and valuable—even if it is annoying and potentially evil. When I get home, I'll just give it back to Mom.

Leaving the restroom, take two. The little toddler is crying that he is going to pee in his pants, and his mom gives me a dirty look as she hurries him into the bathroom.

I hope he makes it. If he doesn't, chalk up another misfortune to the Mirror.

When I get in line to order, I realize the girl Hunter and I insulted is behind the counter taking orders. She's got the same dark eye makeup she was wearing the other day—and her personality doesn't seem any happier.

"What can I get you today?" she asks, giving me the same pained half smile she bestowed on the man in front of me.

Either the girl doesn't remember my nasty remark or she didn't like the guy in front of me too much either. But *I* remember what I said, and I still feel bad about it.

"A large skinny mocha," I say.

"Name?"

I open my mouth to give her a fake name, but stop. If I'm going to take back being the real Rosamunde White Charming, it has to start now.

"Rosie."

She calls out my order while writing my name on the cup.

"That'll be five dollars and ninety cents," she says.

I hand over my money and say, "By the way . . . I'm sorry. For what I said the other day."

"What did you say?" she says without even looking up from the register.

I'm embarrassed to have to repeat it. I don't want to admit that I said those things.

"Um . . . I asked Hunter if he would vote for you for Miss Teen America, and he laughed and he said you looked like a crow . . . Then I said something not nice. And . . . I'm sorry."

She finally looks at me, still holding my change in her hand.

"Oh . . . yeah. You were with that tall sports bro, who normally comes in with his soccer crew and orders a big iced mocha."

I nod, slowly, my cheeks flushing with remorse.

"Out of curiosity, what made you decide to apologize to someone you don't even know?" she asks, dumping the change into my hand.

"I just felt bad because it . . . wasn't the real me," I tell her.

She looks behind me. The line has started to grow while I've been apologizing.

"Apology accepted, real Rosie," she says, shrugging, and for the first time a corner of her mouth turns up in what might be the start of the beginning of a smile. Then, turning to the next person in line, she asks, "What can I get you today?"

I pick up my big skinny mocha, and luckily there's an empty comfortable chair near the window.

Looking out, I see an elderly couple walking past—well, more like shuffling, because they're pretty ancient, and they're taking tiny little old-people steps. But even though they have white hair and wrinkled faces, they are holding hands as they do their old folks shuffle, and they smile at each other with their eyes.

That's what true love looks like, I realize. *That's a real life tale.*

I watch as they cross the street and disappear around the corner, their liver-spotted hands still clasped, and remember the final lines of Elizabeth Barrett Browning's "Sonnet 43":

I love thee with the breath,
Smiles, tears, of all my life; and, if God choose,
I shall but love thee better after death.

It makes so much more sense to me than Romeo and Juliet killing themselves when they barely knew each other.

I take out my Language Arts notebook to write down this insight for Mrs. Minnich.

Elizabeth Barrett Browning understood love better than Shakespeare or Edgar Allen Poe. I don't think Juliet killed herself because she was so in love—at least not real, true love. She was confused. Everyone kept telling her she had to be beautiful and get married when she was still only a teenager. I mean, she still had a nurse! Then handsome Romeo comes along and starts complimenting her—in iambic pentameter, no less—and he becomes the convenient focus for all of her confusion and longing.

As for Poe's "Annabel Lee" narrator—he's more in love with the *idea* of Annabel than the girl herself. She becomes the symbol of the joy and innocence of his childhood instead of a real person with thoughts and ideas of her own.

I hope that's not how all men think about women when they're in love. I mean, it's common (and deeply embarrassing) knowledge that Dad kissed Mom when she was passed out, because he was so overcome by her beauty, but I know for certain that he loves her for deeper reasons now. He always talks about how smart she is, and no one is more proud than Dad when Mom arranges a new deal for CharmingLifestyles.com.

Even if Mom and Dad might have started off with Shakespeare or Poe love, it's developed into Elizabeth Barrett Browning love. Mom doesn't care that her Prince Charming wears readers. She says they make him look brainy and distinguished.

I can totally see Mom and Dad taking tiny old-people steps off into the sunset, holding hands like the elderly couple I saw on the street. That's the happily ever after I want.

"That's a very heavy sigh. Homework?"

I look up and see Mystery Shakespeare Boy standing

next to the empty chair opposite me, holding a large cup of something hot. He's wearing a leather jacket and a T-shirt that says *I'm Just a Poe Boy from a Poe Family*.

"Not exactly. Just some thoughts on . . ."—I don't want to say "love"—"poetry."

"Huh. Mind if I join you?"

"Oh, you recognized me this time?"

A pale wash of pink floods his cheeks.

"I guess I was a little harsh the other day, huh?"

"A little. But maybe a little right, too."

He leans forward, his elbows on his knees and his chin in his hands.

"So . . . at the risk of saying the wrong thing again . . . and possibly being un-PC . . . can I ask what prompted the radical change in appearance in the first place?"

I don't want to lie, because I'm trying to be the real me, but I'm not sure I want to tell him the truth either.

"It's . . . a long story," I say, hoping that will be enough.

"It's okay. I like stories," he says, settling back in his chair. "I'm ready when you are."

So, I tell him about the Fall Festive—how I didn't have a date and against all my better judgment, I asked my mother, who runs a beauty and lifestyle website, for advice on how to get one. And she sent me to Phillipe, and I ended up looking like this.

"It's not like *this* is bad," he says. "It's just *different*."

"Everything is different now," I sigh.

I try to figure out how to explain the situation honestly, but without telling him everything. I don't want to tell him who my parents are, because that either freaks people out or impresses them a little too much. I definitely don't want to mention the talking mirror, because then he'll think I'm completely all-out *loco*.

"It's just that it feels like Mom's solution to the date problem ended up creating more problems. My two best friends aren't talking to me, because Katie thinks I flirted with her boyfriend, Quinn, so he would ask me to the dance when he'd already asked her, but I didn't, I swear," I tell him, looking into his eyes, pleading for the belief that Katie and Nicole didn't give me. "Katie's my best friend. You don't do that to friends."

He shakes his head, and I grip the armrest and look down at my white knuckles. He doesn't believe me either.

"No, I can't see the girl who thought Romeo was an 'emo drama queen' who fell in and out of love too easily doing that to her best friend," he says.

When I look up at him, he's smiling at me, and as

if to make it seem more like a tale of my own, the sun breaks through the clouds in the sky, sending one of its rays down through the canyon of the New York City buildings and into the window of Starcups to bathe us in its glow. I'm serious. I know it sounds like something corny out of a movie, but it's true.

The fact that he believes me gives me the confidence to tell him what's really bothering me.

"The worst part of all this is that I don't like what I see when I look in the Mirror," I confess. "Well, no . . . It's not even that. It's only been a week, but I keep being told I'm supposed to be and do all these different things in order to get a date, and . . . the thing is . . . I'm not sure I know who I *am* anymore."

"I don't know who you are either," he says with a wry grin. "You never told me your name."

"Oh . . . I'm Rosamunde," I tell him. "But my friends call me Rosie."

"And I'm Benjamin, in case you were wondering," he says. "But my friends call me Ben."

"I've been thinking of you as Mystery Shakespeare Boy," I confess.

Ben is in the middle of taking a sip of coffee and does a spit take out of his mouth and nose onto his jeans.

"Nice," I say, handing him a napkin.

"Next time, give me a beverage alert if you're going to say something like that while I'm drinking," Ben says, cutely flustered as he blots the coffee from his pants.

"Sorry," I apologize, but I'm secretly happy to hear him say "next time."

"*Mystery Shakespeare Boy* . . . I like it. Especially the *mystery* part," he says. "Well, really, especially the part that you were thinking about me at all."

Now it's my turn to be flustered. I look out the window, unable to meet his gaze. There's a lady who Mom would probably say "needs to make more of an effort" walking a cute fluffy white dog, who is wearing an outfit that would meet the approval of even the most discerning CharmingLifestyles.com reader. Even Phillipe would have raptures over this dog's adorable little number, complete with matching leash and doggy beret. I wonder what the Mirror would say to the lady if I gave it to her. Would it tell her to get herself together so she could be the Fairest in the Land? Would it be all:

Listen, Dog Lady, look in my glass.
How did you let this mess come to pass?
If you spend all your money on your pup,
Your own love life never will look up!

OMG! I'm starting to think like the Mirror, assuming this lady I know nothing about doesn't have a love life because she's not wearing the most fashionable clothes, but her dog is. For all I know, she's in the most romantic relationship ever, and she and her beloved go shopping for cute little dog outfits together, because that's their thing.

"You're not thinking about me now," Ben says. "What's going on in Rosamunde *my friends call me Rosie*'s head?"

I bring myself back inside the coffee shop. To Ben. To this, whatever it is, that is new and exciting, but scary, too. "I'm thinking about how I've started judging people," I tell him. "But for all the wrong reasons."

"Including yourself?" he asks.

"I guess so," I admit.

"So . . . besides causing lots of problems, did this whole *transform Rosie* thing achieve the objective?" Ben asks. "I mean . . . do you have a date for the dance?"

I give a rueful chuckle.

"I did . . . until earlier today, when I told my date I couldn't go with him."

Ben looks confused. I don't blame him. That makes two of us.

"But . . . I thought the whole point of . . . this"—he

waves his hand in the direction of my hair and clothes—"was to get a date for the dance."

"It was," I sigh. "But what's the point of having a date that you can only communicate with by being mean to other people?"

I know the second Ben makes the connection by the look on his face.

"Wait. . . . Your date for the dance is *soccer guy*?!"

"*Was* my date. Isn't anymore."

"Whew!" Ben says. "Although, I still can't believe he ever was in the first place."

"Desperation makes Rosie do stupid things, I guess."

"So . . . you don't have a date now?"

"No," I sigh. "I'm back to square one. Being a date-less loser."

He puts his coffee cup down and leans forward.

"So, Rosie, two things. Thing one: It's easy to change who you see when you look in the mirror if you don't recognize the person you see," he says. "You already did that once, right? Why can't you do it again?"

"Funny you should mention that," I say, pulling the box of hair color out of my bag.

"Great minds," he chuckles.

"So . . . what's thing two?"

He hesitates, looking down at his coffee-spotted knees, and then back at me with a surprisingly shy smile.

"Thing two: If you need a date for the dance . . . well, I can dance. Kind of. I'm not going to win any competitions, unless it's for best funky chicken, and . . . I know I'm no Prince Charming, but . . ."

If he only knew how totally awkward it would be if he *were* Prince Charming!

"I would love to go to the dance with you," I tell him. "Because now I *really* want to see this funky chicken."

Ben laughs.

"You might wish you never said that," he says. "The funky chicken part, I mean. Hopefully not the part about wanting to go to the dance with me."

No, that part I can't seeing myself regretting, not the way I did with Hunter. That part, unlike pretty much everything else that has happened in the last ten days, feels just right.

Chapter Twelve

I PRACTICALLY FLOAT HOME FROM STAR-cups, feeling better than I have since Mom gave me the Mirror.

"Good afternoon, Miss Rosie," Victor says as he opens the door for me.

"It *is* a good afternoon, isn't it, Victor?" I say, stopping to give him a hug.

He's taken aback by my sudden display of affection—I haven't given him hugs since I was little.

"I'm glad to hear that, Miss Rosie," Victor says, patting me on the back. "You've seemed . . . not quite yourself lately."

"Don't worry," I tell him. "That's about to change."

"Good," he says. "Because Rosie Charming is pretty special, if you ask me."

And he digs into the pocket of his coat as if he's about to get me a Tootsie Roll and then hesitates. "What's your current policy on Tootsie Rolls, Miss Rosie?"

"I'm definitely firmly in the Pro Tootsie Roll Camp at this particular moment," I say.

"I'm happy to hear that," he says, digging one out of his pocket and dropping it into my waiting hand.

"Thanks, Victor," I say, and then head upstairs to work on my transformation from Mirror Girl back to Rosie.

The first step is the box of hair color. I've never used it before. It says to do a little test area and wait twenty-four hours to see if you have a reaction, but no way am I going to bother with that. I can't wait that long to be real Rosie. I mix the color and the accelerator together and carefully apply it to my hair, trying not to get it on the bathroom counter or my clothes. I set the timer on my cell for ten minutes and then take the Mirror compact out of my backpack.

I'm going to give it back to Mom when she gets home from her meeting with "some high level CynCorp executives to discuss the rollout of the Fairest Mirrors line."

I wonder if any of the designs in Mom's new line will be based on this one, I think, rubbing the jewels with the bottom of my shirt so their colors glow even more beautifully in the lamplight.

Deep down, I know it's a mistake for me to open the compact again. That Shrimpy and Harold are right and nothing good can come from this object, even if it is a family heirloom made of fine gold that is heavy in my hand, and flawless jewels from the Seven Mountains Mine that are worth a fortune. But it calls to me. It's like that friend that you know will end up saying something mean, but you keep doing stuff with them thinking *this time it'll be different.*

I can feel my heart beating faster as I open the compact and look at myself in the Mirror. I definitely don't look anything like the Fairest in the Land with dark hair coloring smeared all over my scalp. But that doesn't matter to me, even if it does to the Mirror.

Mirror, Mirror, in my hand,
I don't care if I'm Fairest in the Land
As long as to my Self I'm true
And so, I say good-bye to you.

The compact heats up and vibrates in my hand. I

almost close it, but then I decide to let the Mirror have its say. I can take it.

Ungrateful Princess, you little fool,
You could have reigned over all the school.
You could have been Fairest, number one,
But now you're just like everyone.

"Whatever," I say, snapping the compact shut. "At least I'm not just a bitter piece of talking glass."

The buzzer goes off on my cell, and I get into the shower and rinse my hair. When I get out, I throw on a pair of my old jeans and a *Read More Books* T-shirt and throw all the makeup from Phillipe into the trash.

After I dry my hair, I take a selfie and text it to Katie and Nicole.

"Please respond," I whisper as I press send.

Nicole does, right away.

OMG! What happened to the new hair?

I decided I liked the old me better, I text back.

What does your mom say?

She hasn't seen it yet, I text.

O . . . o!!!! Nicole texts. *PS. I like the old you better too.*

Just then Kate responds in the group text.

Me three!

Can we video chat? I write. *I have NEWZ!*

They agree, and we move to video.

"So . . . what's the big news, besides you changing your hair back to normal?" Katie asks.

"I told Hunter I'm not going to the dance with him," I say.

The shock on both of their faces is comical.

"But . . . all you've been talking about is getting a date for the dance, and now you finally got one, and you tell him you don't want to go?" Nicole says. "What is with you?"

"Wait . . . Quinn didn't ask you again, did he?" Katie asks, suddenly suspicious.

"NO!" I exclaim. "And if he did, I'd say no *again*."

"So, are you not going now?" Nicole asks. "Because I thought you did the whole makeover thing because you wanted to go to the Fall Festive."

"I did," I admit. "And I *am* going to the Fall Festive. Just not with Hunter and just not as madeover Rosie."

"Okay, now I'm totally confused," Katie says. "Can anyone explain to me what is going on?"

"I can't," Nicole grumbles. "Because I'm just as baffled as you are. Who, exactly, are you going to the dance with?"

"Mystery Shakespeare Boy," I tell them. "Except his real name is Ben."

They both look clueless.

"You remember, the guy I met at Starcups the day I had the appointment with Phillipe? We argued about *Romeo and Juliet*?"

It comes back to Katie first.

"You're going to the dance with the rando from Starcups?!" she practically shouts. "Are you *crazy*?!"

"He's not a rando!" I retort. "He's a nice, funny guy named Ben."

"Are you sure about this?" Nicole asks. "I mean, you hardly even know him."

Katie thinks she knows Quinn, but he asked me to the dance behind her back. Mom hardly knew Dad when he kissed her in the glass coffin, which, I have to add, I still think is major league creepy, but despite the weird beginning, their relationship has stood the test of time. The Tale makes it sound like it's all about love at first sight and Mom's beauty and Dad's handsomeness, but that's not the real story. What makes for the happily ever after is how they respect each other and know how to laugh together. How they're a real team.

"It's just a date for a dance, guys, it's not like we're

getting *married*," I point out. "Look, my mom went riding off into the sunset with Dad after he'd kissed her *when he thought she was dead.* Being attracted to randos must be in my DNA or something."

Nicole and Katie don't say anything for a second or two, and I wonder if they think I'm crazy. But then they both burst out laughing.

"I've missed you, Rosie," Katie says.

"Can you guys come over tomorrow after school?" I ask. "I need your help looking for a dress for the dance. I want to hit the thrift stores."

What I don't tell them is that I plan to give them all of the clothes Phillipe picked out for me at Très Cher. I don't need or want them anymore. They're a skin I have to shed—Mirror Girl's uniform.

"Now I know the old Rosie is back!" Katie says.

"Sounds like a plan," Nicole agrees.

Just then I hear the front door and Mom calling, "Rosie! I'm home!"

"Got to go," I tell them. "See you tomorrow."

I take the compact and search out my mother. She's in the kitchen making herself a cup of CharmingLifestyles SilverNeedle White Tea: *soothes while it smooths—antiaging blend!*

Mom's teaspoon clatters to the counter.

"Rosamunde White Charming! What have you done to your hair?"

Oops. I'd forgotten about that in my haste to give her back the Mirror.

"I dyed it back to normal," I say.

"But . . . *why?*" Mom asks. "Do you realize how much a cut and color with Giacomo costs?"

I hadn't really thought about that, to be honest, and I feel bad about wasting Mom's money on the color.

"I'm sorry, Mom," I say. "It's just . . . I didn't feel like me anymore."

I hold out the compact.

"I want to give this back to you. It's . . . not a good thing for me to have."

Mom doesn't take it from me right away, so I'm left holding it, arm outstretched, fingers trembling.

"Come, sit down and tell me why," Mom says. "Do you want some tea?"

"No, thanks," I say. I just want to get the Mirror out of my hand and into hers.

Mom brings her cup to the kitchen table, and I bring the Mirror compact. Since Mom seems in no hurry to take it from me, I place it on the table between us. The diamonds in the cover wink up at us under the kitchen lights.

"So, why don't you think this is good for you?" Mom says, pointing to the Mirror.

"First, can you answer a question? Is the Mirror in there part of . . . you know, *the* Mirror? Stepgrandmother's Mirror?"

Mom smiles.

"So, you figured that out. I thought you would."

"Wait, you *knew* you were giving me a piece of that crazy Mirror?" I exclaim. "Why would you do that?" I'm having a hard time getting my head around the fact that my own mother *knowingly* gave me a piece of a psychopathic glass. "I mean, that thing made Stepgrandma try to *kill* you! What if it had made me into a teenage serial killer?"

"I gave it to you because I believe in you," Mom says, which makes everything as clear as mud.

"What?"

My mother takes a sip of tea before responding.

"If I just told you what I've learned from living my life, you wouldn't listen," Mom explains. "I didn't listen to your uncles when they told me not to talk to strangers. I thought I knew everything. I thought I knew better than they did. I was a Princess of the Royal Blood and they were Little People."

"But Harold said you weren't a snob—you were nice to everyone at the Castle," I say, confused. "He said that's the real reason he didn't kill you. Not because of your beauty, like they say in The Tale."

"I might have been nice on the outside, but inside . . . Well, I was just as much of a snob as the next princess," Mom admits.

"So, what has this got to do with giving me the Mirror?"

"I wanted you to learn for yourself that being the Fairest in the Land isn't all it's cracked up to be," Mom explains. "I knew that you would have the strength of character not to give in to the Mirror's enticements the way my stepmother did."

"But how could you know for sure?" I ask. "I'm confused about pretty much everything at the moment."

"I didn't. There was always a tiny bit of doubt that you might succumb. But I was keeping a close eye on the situation in case you did." She looks at me, and her eyes are dewy. "I knew my daughter would take the things she needed to learn from the Mirror and then do what I did— lock it away until it was time to give it to her daughter."

"So, what did *you* learn from the Mirror?" I ask Mom.

"Before you locked it away and gave it to me?"

Mom trails a manicured nail over the jewels on the cover of the compact.

"The Mirror gave me confidence—the confidence that I use today when I go in to a meeting with CynCorp executives and negotiate a multimillion-dollar deal," Mom says. "And, let's face it—the Mirror also gave me The Tale. Without the Mirror I wouldn't have met your father, and I wouldn't have had you."

She takes my hand and squeezes it.

"And you, darling, are always the Fairest to Dad and me, no matter what the Mirror says."

"Even with the ten-dollar box color?" I ask.

Mom smiles. "Even then. . . . But next time you feel like a color change, promise you'll let me send you to a professional?"

How can I argue with that?

"You know, we owe the Mirror something else," Mom says.

"What's that?" I ask.

"All this," she says, waving her arm around at our beautiful kitchen inside our lovely apartment in a luxury prewar doorman building on the Upper East Side of Manhattan.

Shaking my head, I ask, "What does the Mirror have to do with our apartment?"

"Not just the apartment, Rosie. Our lifestyle. Our family. Your father and I built the CharmingLifestyles brand around The Tale—and without the Mirror, there wouldn't be a story to tell."

Mom's right. I mean, look at the latest deal she put together for the Fairest range of mirrors. I owe my future college education to that annoying piece of bitter talking glass on the table.

"I guess you're right," I admit. "But it caused so many problems. Quinn Fairchild asked me to the dance, even though he'd already asked Katie, and then Katie didn't believe me when I said I didn't flirt with him, and she and Nicole weren't talking to me, and Nicole said I'd changed but not in a good way, and—"

"Oh please, you think *you* had it bad?" Mom says. "At least I didn't tell Harold the Huntsman to take you into Central Park, kill you, and bring me your heart so I could eat it."

I stare at her and then start laughing hysterically. Because when you look at it that way, I did get off pretty easily. I didn't have to choke on a poisoned apple either, so Dad and I can keep going to the diner for apple pie.

Mom finishes her tea and stands up, taking the Mirror with her.

"I'll go put this back in the safe," she says.

"Good," I tell her.

As she leaves the room, I send the Mirror a final good-bye in my thoughts:

Mirror, Mirror, getting locked away

Till my daughter is born, maybe someday.

What she'll learn from you, we'll have to see.

Just be nicer to her than you were to me.

Chapter Thirteen

OKAY, I LIED.

I gave Katie the flowery skirt she loved and Nicole the lace dress, and I donated *most* of the makeup to our local shelter. But the truth is, I kept a few of the cool lip glosses. And the brown eye pencil that made my eyes look bigger and smoky when I smudged it. And I didn't give *all* the clothes away. I kept the awesome leather jacket and a funky pair of boots.

I tried to figure out which parts of Phillipe's makeover made me feel good but still like me. Real Rosie me, not Mirror Girl. I kept those parts and threw the rest away, like a crab abandoning a shell or a snake shedding unwanted skin.

Now I've got to find my new skin, which is why I'm at the thrift store with Nicole and Katie, looking for a dress for the Fall Festive.

"What about this?" Katie says, holding up a gold sequined sheath. "I love it!"

Mirror Girl would love it too. It's eye-catching. It's a *center of attention* dress.

But I've had enough of that in the last week or two. I want something more low-key. A little more . . . me.

I shake my head.

"Ooh, what about this one?" Nicole says, pulling a black flapper dress with a gold fringed hemline off the rack.

I hold it up to me and look in the mirror. It's cool and different, but it's just not singing my song.

"I like it, but . . . I don't know. Let's keep looking," I say.

We keep sifting through the racks, dress by dress, until I see it. The perfect one.

"This is it!" I say.

It's a strapless '50s number with a white chiffon skirt with wide petticoats and a blue lace fitted top. I'm in love.

Praying that it fits, I go into the changing room to try it on.

As I zip it up, I close my eyes, afraid to look in the mirror, afraid that I'll hear someone else's voice in my head.

It fits.

I open my eyes and look in the mirror. I feel like a princess. I feel like the Fairest in the Land, even though I'm in a thrift store changing room in a party dress and Converse. But best of all, I still feel like me.

I let Mom take me for a mani-pedi the day of the Fall Festive but draw the line at getting my hair done.

"I still don't understand why you had to ruin perfectly good professional highlights with a ten-dollar box color job," Mom grumbles.

"I wanted to be normal again," I explain for the umpteenth time.

"But why does that involve using a home hair color kit?" Mom asks. "You can still be yourself with professional highlights."

"Being the Fairest in the Land is your thing, Mom. You're really good at it. Maybe I'm just cut out for other things."

"You're beautiful, Rosie," Mom says. "And beauty is power. Don't you see? It's not fair, but that's why you have to make the best of yourself. CharmingLifestyles.com has been successful because we help people do that."

It's like I'm hearing the voice of Mirror Girl speaking to me through my mother's mouth. Does Mom have her own Mirror Girl? Maybe everyone does.

"I'm trying to be beautiful in my own way, Mom, okay? What's the matter with that?"

Mom, who always seems to have an answer to everything, can't seem to find the words to answer that question.

"You'll understand when you're older," she sighs, finally. "Life isn't as simple as you think it is when you're a kid. Society has rules. Expectations."

"So, why can't we change them?" I ask. "If they're wrong, I mean."

Mom looks at me, and for the first time, I notice the fine lines around her eyes. But I also notice the deep love for me there.

"Rosie, you keep on being you, honey. Because you are beautiful, no matter what you see in the mirror."

I hug my mother, careful not to ruin either of our manicures, and feel closer to her than I have in a long time.

As I'm getting dressed for the Fall Festive, I feel like a princess in a fairy tale. Yeah, I know. With my parentage it's even more cliché, but when I put on the dress, it makes me feel like anything is possible. I bought some blue silk ribbon to match the lace on the bodice, and I tie it like a headband, leaving the rest of my hair falling straight down my back. Slipping on the new pair of white Converse I bought to match it, I twirl in front of the mirror, and the chiffon skirt floats in a wide circle around me, drifting against my legs like a soft cloud when I stop.

The doorbell rings. Mystery Shakespeare Boy—I mean, Ben—is here. Dad is answering the door. I better go rescue Ben from the Charming Inquisition. I finally had to fess up to him who my parents are.

"So, Ben, tell me. What are your plans for this evening?" I hear my father asking from down the hall.

I walk faster.

"Uh . . . well, um . . . Mr. Charming, er . . . Prince . . . sir, my plan is to take Rosie to her school dance."

"And . . . ?"

I can just imagine the intimidating look on Dad's face right now. I run, reaching the doorway before Ben can answer.

"Don't worry, Dad, Ben isn't going to kiss me while I'm sleeping or anything," I say. "Right, Ben?"

My father gives me a stern frown. Ben, on the other hand, is looking at me like he's never seen me before. Like everyone always looked at Mirror Girl. Like I'm really beautiful.

"Wow, Rosie. You look really . . . Wow. Love the dress."

For some reason, this causes Dad to frown even more.

Ben holds out a bunch of blush tea roses, which is appropriate since he is blushing pretty hard himself. "I . . . uh . . . got these for you. Hope the rose thing isn't too cliché, but they reminded me of you."

"No, they're beautiful," I tell him.

Just then Mom sweeps out from the kitchen.

"Ben—wonderful to meet you," she says, holding out her soft, white hand.

Ben looks like he isn't sure if he should shake it or kiss it. Fortunately, he decides to shake it.

"Y-you t-too Mrs. White—er, Charming."

People often start stuttering in Mom's presence. I'm used to her face, but other people find it intimidating— too beautiful to be real.

"Ivan, can you please stop glowering at Ben and do something useful like take pictures?" Mom says pointedly to Dad, who is indeed a standing column of granite, giving Ben his full range of Intimidating Princely Looks.

Dad harrumphs and goes off in search of his camera—or at least I hope it's his camera and not his CharmingMaster 15 Recurve Bow.

"Don't mind him," Mom says to Ben. "He can be a little overprotective."

"A little?" I snort.

"Why don't you go put those lovely roses in water?" Mom suggests. "I'll keep Ben company."

She's clearly trying to get Ben alone so she can ask him twenty questions, but I can't say "Not on your life, Mom" without making a scene.

So, I race into the kitchen, find a plastic water jug, and stuff the roses in without even taking the plastic off.

"Sorry, flowers," I whisper. "I promise to sort you out after the dance. Right now I have to rescue Ben."

"So, you met Rosie at Starcups, you say?" Mom's asking Ben as I walk back in from the kitchen.

"Yes, and we were both awake at the time—discussing Shakespeare, as a matter of fact," I point out, quite pointedly, if you must know.

"Er, yes. . . . It was *Romeo and Juliet*," Ben says. He sounds odd, like he has a cough lozenge stuck in his throat.

Luckily, Dad comes back just then with his camera,

rather than hunting or siege equipment. Mom fusses about where we should stand to get the right lighting.

"Mom, it would be great if we could actually leave for the Fall Festive before it's over," I grumble.

"You'll thank me for this in twenty years when you have a great picture to share with your children," Mom says.

She didn't just say that.

I can't even look at Ben, but he's got to be blushing just like I am. Our hypothetical children are going to see a picture of two tomato-faced people who are, like, *Please just take the picture and let us get to the dance already!*

Dad takes a bunch of pictures, and I've finally had enough.

"Okay, time to go!" I declare.

"Just one more," Dad says.

"No! No more!" I say. "Paparazzi hour is over."

"You two have a lovely evening," Mom says.

"We will," I say, anxious to get Ben away from Dad's less than Charming glare and Mom's apparent matrimonial plans soon as as possible.

"Wait, Rosie—" Mom says as Ben and I are walking out the door. "You can't possibly be thinking of wearing those sneakers to the dance with that dress. . . ."

"Yeah, Mom, I can," I reply, blowing her and Dad a kiss and closing the door behind us.

Ben and I don't say a word to each other until we get into the elevator and the door closes. And then we just start cracking up. Laughing and laughing so hard my eyes start watering and I'm afraid the brown eye pencil is going to go from artfully smudged to tackily smeared.

"When you said the thing about kissing your mom while she was sleeping . . . ," Ben gasped. "I almost lost it."

"You looked terrified," I said. "I figured it would lighten the mood."

"I *was* terrified," Ben admits. "Your dad scares the heck out of me."

"He's actually quite Charming when you get to know him," I say, which cracks Ben up even more.

Victor is on doorman duty.

"You're a sight for sore eyes, Miss Rosie," he says. "If I were fifty years younger, I'd take you to the dance myself."

"Thanks, Victor," I say.

"I'll do my best to fill in for you, sir," Ben says.

"You do that, young man," Victor says. "Dance a cha-cha for me."

When we get out on the sidewalk, Ben admits he doesn't know what the cha-cha entails, but he's happy to google it if I want to try it.

"That's okay," I tell him. "I'll settle for something you don't have to google."

The cafeteria is decked out in fall colors—leaf cutouts in red, orange, gold, and brown adorn tree trunks that have been taped to the walls, and there are hay bales and corn sheaves and huge pumpkins arranged artfully around the room to complete the Fall Festive motif. There's hot apple cider and every kind of pumpkin and apple flavored baked treat you could possibly imagine.

Katie is already there with Jackson Greenleaf, whom she asked to go with her after learning that Quinn had asked me. They live in the same building and have been friends since nursery school, when her mother almost had heart failure from finding little Jackson on the ledge outside their apartment, ten stories up. He'd climbed out of his window on the fifth floor, up the fire escape, and along the ledge.

Besides being a friend, Jackson fits Katie's qualifications—he's cute and they'll look good in pictures together. Plus, he can dance, she says.

My date meets those qualifications too. Okay, I haven't seen him dance yet. But he looks great in his suit, tie, and Converse, and he's a lot of fun to be with.

The DJ starts playing "Happy," and Ben says, "They're playing our song."

I didn't know it was our song, but as of right now, it is.

We head out onto the dance floor, and Ben starts moving in what is a hilarious approximation of dancing. His long, lanky body seems to move in every direction at once in a way that is disjointed, but somehow matches the beat of the music perfectly. He looks like . . .

"OMG, you really *are* a funky chicken!" I laugh.

"I told you!" he says, smiling from ear to ear. "With me, there is complete truth in advertising."

Ben's the opposite of a CynCorp ad. What you see really is what you get.

Maybe that's why I like him. And I do. Like him, that is.

Although right now, I'm being careful to stay out of the way of his flailing arms and legs as he dances.

Is he my Prince Charming? It's too early to tell. Besides, it's only our first date, I'm in eighth grade, and I never bought into the *love at first sight* thing.

For now it's enough that he's honest, he likes me the way I am, he's fun to be with—and he does a mean funky chicken.

Acknowledgments

THE BEST TEACHERS DON'T TELL YOU what to do; they ask you the right questions so you figure it out yourself. This book is dedicated to Cindy Minnich because she did just that: Her question gave me the flash of insight that finally let me tell a story I'd first conceived of over ten years ago, and tried writing (unsuccessfully) several different ways. Morals of this story: 1) Surround yourself with smart people who ask good questions, and 2) If at first you don't succeed, try, try again. And again. And again.

I am so incredibly grateful to have the support and friendship of superagent Jennifer Laughran, the Sisterhood of the Brass Necklace, and my fellow retreaters at Kindling Words East and Swinger of Birches. Without you I would collapse into a reclusive pile of insecure goop. Also, my life would be considerably less fun.

Thank you to the wonderful team at Simon & Schuster/Aladdin for seeing the possibilities in this book: my lovely editor, Alyson Heller; production editor, Mandy Veloso; designer, Laura Lyn DiSiena; and illustrator, Angela Navarra, for the gorgeous cover art.

Most of all, thank you to my beloved family, especially my older female relatives, who taught me what it means to be a strong woman. Also to my greatest loves, Hank, Josh, and Amie, to whom I hope I give the benefit of this knowledge.

This is the last book of mine that my mother, Susan Darer, read in manuscript form before she passed away suddenly and unexpectedly in March 2015. I still hear her voice in my head every day. It is a much better influence than the Mirror.

ABOUT THE AUTHOR

Sarah Darer Littman is the critically acclaimed author of *Backlash*; *Want to Go Private?*; *Life, After*; *Purge*; and *Confessions of a Closet Catholic*, winner of the Sydney Taylor Book Award. When she's not writing novels, Sarah is an award-winning columnist for the online news site CTNewsJunkie, and she teaches creative writing as an adjunct professor in the MFA program at Western Connecticut State University. Visit her online at sarahdarerlittman.com.